CHEERING THE COWBOY

Grape Seed Falls Romance Book 7, Royal Brothers Book 3

LIZ ISAACSON

ISBN-13: 978-1983223938

CHAPTER ONE

Austin Royal washed his hands with the best mechanic's soap available, but the faint black lines of grease never really left his skin. It would have to be enough. He was already late, and there was nothing that made him jumpier than walking into church after the sermon had started. Something his parents had engrained in him since he was a boy.

He took a few precious seconds to smooth his beard, thinking it had come in quite nicely despite what his brothers said. Then he swiped his cowboy hat from the dresser in his bedroom and headed downstairs.

He shared the homestead with his oldest brother, Shane, and his wife, Robin. They'd been married for about three months now, and everyone had worked out a system to keep from stepping on each other's toes.

Dylan had taken over Robin's tiny house, a two hundred and eight square foot home that she'd parked way down on the end of Cabin Row, where Dylan spent most of his time anyway. He'd built one new cabin already, and had the skeleton of another going up. He worked with the cattle on the ranch the brothers had bought six months ago, and he was halfway through remodeling the home Austin would eventually move into.

Austin grabbed his keys from the hook by the door in the kitchen. "Goin' to church," he called, not really sure where everyone else was at the moment. Someone yelled back to him, and he skipped down the few steps in the garage to one of the trucks they owned.

He was happier than he'd ever been since being forced to leave his family's ranch just outside of San Antonio. He'd just celebrated his thirty-third birthday. By all accounts, Austin should be laughing while he counted his blessings.

But a vein of anger existed in him he didn't know how to deal with. Always there, always just seething right below the surface, the negativity felt like a black plague on his soul. He'd been trying to get to church every week, and sometimes that helped. But he was starting to suspect that it wasn't enough, that nothing would able be able to cure him from this darkness he felt inside himself.

He kept the music off as he drove, using the thirty-minute drive to mentally run through his upcoming week. He craved this solitude, as he'd been working with the three ranch hands that had come with Triple Towers when he and his brothers had bought it.

Oaker and Carlos were friendly enough. They'd educated all the brothers about where things were and how things were done. Shane had changed almost all of it, because the ranch was in complete disrepair, both physically and financially.

Dylan had taken care of the outbuildings. Together, he and Shane were working on the pasture rotations, getting more hay planted, and dealing with all the legal rights with the water on the ranch. Austin had been tasked with all the horse care—which wasn't much, considering they had four horses.

Shane had brought one over from Grape Seed Ranch, where the brothers used to work, and Dylan and his fiancée, Hazel, and Austin had purchased a horse each from Levi Rhodes. Austin loved horses and didn't mind the time it took to care for them. Robin, who was a professional farrier, did quite a bit to keep them shod and healthy too.

Austin's real love, surprisingly, came with the huge hen house that had come with the ranch. Shane had wanted to sell the chickens and knock down the coop in favor of something else. But Austin had taken a liking to the clucking, the methodical gathering of eggs, and the seemingly constant need to feed the beasts.

With one hundred and four chickens to care for, Austin spent a lot of time in that coop. It had become his sanctuary of sorts, and he wasn't sure if he should chuckle at that or take the fact of the matter to his grave.

When he wasn't doing those tasks, he worked with Shayleigh in the equipment shed, thus the grease stains in his fingerprints. She'd been an Army mechanic, and while she was as beautiful as an angel, she had the disposition of a cornered wildcat.

He got along best with her out of anyone, so he'd been enduring hours with her in the afternoon, under her rough hand of correction, his patience thinning by the day. She went to the same church as him, but he deliberately didn't ask her to drive in with him, nor did he sit by her. He'd asked—once.

The look of disdain she'd given him had been scathing enough to remind him each week that she was not interested. Fine by him. He needed the thirty minutes in and the thirty minutes back to re-center himself anyway. And her presence was anything but centering.

He arrived in plenty of time to park where he wanted and sit on the far right side the way he liked. Sometimes a couple of cowboys he knew from other ranches and farms surrounding the town of Grape Seed Falls sat by him, but today, the crowd was thin.

Didn't matter. Austin needed to be there, even if it was just him and the minister.

Pastor Gifford got up and said, "Everyone must be home baking pies today," and Austin remembered that it was nearly Thanksgiving. His mother would be joining them on the ranch on the Wednesday before the holiday, and he'd be the one to make sure she got settled. He always was, though Dylan and Shane took care of their mom too.

The pastor spoke about being grateful, accepting help when it was offered, and offering service at this time of year to those who might need it. "Pray for opportunities to serve others," he said. "The Lord can use you. He will use you."

Austin felt like he could barely keep his head above water most days. He didn't get a chance to interact with many people outside the ranch, but he supposed there were still plenty of opportunities to help the ranch hands or his brothers with something. Wasn't there?

After the service ended, Austin stayed in his seat while everyone else filed out. Pastor Gifford would be busy for several minutes, and Austin needed a few minutes before their meeting anyway.

He'd finally plucked up the courage to ask Pastor Gifford for help. Was that why the minister had focused his speech today about accepting help or looking for ways to serve? What if that was all Austin needed to hear?

He closed his eyes and prayed, asking God for guidance, for a way to cleanse himself from his dark thoughts. No definitive answer came, not that Austin was expecting it to.

When there was little noise left coming from the foyer, Austin stood and made his way there. Pastor Gifford saw him and finished saying good-bye to the last couple. "Austin," he said warmly, a smile on his face that felt one-hundred percent genuine. "Let's go talk in my office."

He led the way down a short hall and around the corner before pushing through a thick door and into a decent-sized office. He pulled his tie loose around his neck and sighed as he sat.

"What can I help you with today?" He folded his arms on his desk and looked at Austin expectantly.

Austin removed his cowboy hat and worried his fingers along

the brim. He sat too, wishing the words would magically align themselves. "Well, I'm not really sure...."

"What's bothering you?"

Austin looked at the man, probably close to his father's age. The thought of his father clarified things. "I'm angry," he said. "About a lot of things that shouldn't make me angry. I don't feel... normal. It's always there, and I don't know how to get rid of it."

Pastor Gifford nodded. "Go on."

"I think...I just need to know what to do."

The minister shook his head, though a smaller version of the smile he'd worn in the foyer returned. "I can't tell you what to do." He opened a desk drawer and turned his attention to that. "Let me see...I think I have something you might try."

Austin wanted a pill, maybe some magic beans, anything that would take this feeling away. He leaned forward as Pastor Gifford placed a simple business card on the desk.

"Anger management?" Austin read the card. "Classes, meetings, and more. Thursdays at seven p.m." He looked at the pastor. "You think I should go to anger management classes?"

"I've had several patrons who've attended," he said, nudging the card closer. "They speak highly of the program."

Austin took the card, but it felt too heavy to take home with him. "All right. Thanks." He stood, disappointed, not quite expecting the minister to give him more to do. That well of anger he barely kept contained started boiling, and Austin needed to leave. Now.

He stuffed the card in his back pocket and left the office, then the church. The wind tried to steal his hat from right off the top of his head—another thing to make him angry. The blasted wind. Who got angry over wind?

TIME SEEMED TO MOVE SLOWLY, BUT THURSDAY EVENTUALLY came. He didn't want to tell anyone where he was going, because then they'd want to know why. And he didn't want Shane or Dylan to A. worry, or B. ask him questions, or C. give him advice.

Sure, he knew Shane spoke with a therapist regularly, using an app called Talk To Me. It had done amazing things for Shane's own pent-up anger and feelings of abandonment. Dylan didn't seem to have quite as many problems, but Austin had noticed that he'd stopped talking to their father about a year ago. He seemed happier for it too, and Hazel had really helped in that department as well.

Austin, the youngest, still unattached, was lonely. Angry about being lonely. Sad. Angry about being sad. And most of all, he was completely done with being duped by his dad. That was what made him the angriest, and he decided while he put his horse away on Thursday evening that he would go to the anger management meeting.

He met Robin on his way out of the stable, and seized the opportunity. "Hey, I'm heading into town tonight. Can you tell Shane?"

"Sure." She didn't give him a funny look or question why he'd go into town on a Thursday. Now if he could just get the keys and get out of there....

He managed to do both without seeing anyone except Shay, who had her two German shepherds engaged in some sort of training exercise. Her dogs were beautiful and well-behaved, and she spent serious time making sure of both.

It was barely five-thirty when he arrived in Grape Seed Falls, so Austin bummed around town, got dinner, and finally parked at the library a few minutes before the meeting was set to start. Maybe he could sneak in the back and just listen.

With only two minutes to spare, he got out of the truck and went inside the lower level of the library, where all the meeting rooms were located. Low-level chatter met his ears from a room at the end of the hall, and he slicked his palms down the front of his jeans.

His heart pounded, and he felt like he was walking the plank, heading right for a watery grave. The door stood open and a patch of brighter light fell onto the carpet. The scent of chocolate and something fruity met his nose, but it wasn't comforting the way it had been when his mother had baked cookies for the boys after school.

He paused a few strides away from the door, his mind still warring with itself. He hadn't seen anyone yet, and he could just walk on by. Pretend he'd come to the wrong room. Anything. Something.

Just go inside.

The words entered his mind, erasing and silencing the jumbled mess his thoughts had become.

So he straightened his shoulders and marched toward the room, deciding once and for all that he was not going to let his anger rule his life. Not anymore.

His first step in the room and someone moved right in front of him. He couldn't slow. Couldn't stop. Couldn't dodge.

His instinct kicked in and he had a half-second to brace before he collided with another body. A softer body than his, but still hard in specific places. He grabbed onto her arms—it was a woman with streaked hair. Pink tips.

Something cold and wet seeped through his shirt, and he looked down at his chest.

Punch. Red punch.

"Let go of me." The woman spoke in a near-growl, and Austin hastened to obey her, unsure of when he'd clamped his fingers around her biceps.

Another step back, and all his senses started working again. Eyes. Nose. Ears.

A hush had fallen on the room, and he glanced around to find at least a dozen people in attendance, including the woman he'd barreled straight into

"Shay?" he asked.

She accepted a handful of napkins from another woman and started mopping up her own ruined shirt. She wore a pair of jeans that hugged every feminine curve, the same pair of cowgirl boots he'd seen countless times, and a pretty sea foam green shirt. Well, it used to be pretty. Now with the red stain, it looked like a Christmas nightmare.

"What are you doin' here?" she asked, and not kindly. Her hazel eyes flashed with annoyance, but she didn't look fully at him until she'd thrown away the wad of napkins.

She folded her arms and cocked her hip, and Austin should not have found her so attractive. After all, this was going to be an argument, and he wouldn't walk away the winner. He rarely did with Shayleigh Hatch.

But she was gorgeous, and strong, and feminine all at the same time. He'd sensed a softer Shay under the hard armor she presented to the world, but he hadn't cracked it. Hadn't even tried. Wasn't sure it was worth the effort.

But now, staring at her in this new environment where she couldn't boss him around and couldn't make him feel two inches tall, Austin wondered if the spark he'd always felt between them was really as one-sided as she'd claimed it to be.

So he'd asked her to dance at his brother's wedding. He could admit it. She'd turned him down by laughing in his face and saying she'd never be interested in him. His place with her had been made very clear, and he hadn't tried to move from the corner she'd put him in.

But now.... Now something started to buzz in his bloodstream. Whisper fantasies through his mind. Fan that dormant flame into something brilliant and hot.

"Let it go, Shay," the woman who'd brought her the napkins said, stepping between her and Austin. "It's time to start." She cast a nervous look at Austin that said, *Please just go sit down. Or leave. Something.*

Shay drew in a deep breath through her nose, her glare miraculously dropping in intensity. "Time to start. Right."

She turned away from him, and then twisted back to say, "I think the meeting for men who steal women's ranches is upstairs," in a cold, dismissive tone that made all the parts of Austin that had started to hum quiet.

Especially when Shay rounded the few rows of chairs that had been set up, took her position at the front of the room, and said, "All right, everyone. Welcome to our weekly meeting. It's time to begin."

CHAPTER TWO

S hayleigh Hatch couldn't believe—could not *believe*—that Austin Royal had shown up and spilled punch all over her shirt. A light colored one too—one of her favorites.

And why was he sitting in the back row, his fingers curled into fists and his eyes squarely on her?

Surely he wasn't here for the anger management meeting. But he hadn't left....

His shirt was blue and white plaid, and with the red punch stain, he looked like he was ready for the Fourth of July.

Shay forced herself to focus on the other thirteen people who'd come to the library tonight. Sometimes there were only four or five people in attendance, and she didn't want to drive more people away because she couldn't control her temper.

She'd worked too hard for too long to let a man—even if he was good-looking and charming—like Austin undo her composure.

"Shawna is here to meet with us," Shay said, indicating the dark-skinned woman who had changed Shay's life in the eighteen months since she'd retired from the Army and returned to Grape Seed Falls. "I'll turn the time over to her."

Shay stepped to the side so Shawna could have the floor, and she realized that all the chairs were filled—except for one right beside Austin.

Even her deep breathing wouldn't help the feelings coiling through her now. Besides, sucking in a lungful of air of his delicious cowboy scent would be enough to drive her crazy—a different kind of madness, but madness all the same.

But she couldn't leave. So she walked around the back of the room, intending to just lean against the wall. Austin stood before she'd come all the way to a halt and gestured for her to take the inside seat.

She couldn't very well cause another scene, so she glared as hard and with as much of the fury she felt inside in his direction, not allowing herself to make full eye contact with him. It didn't matter. She didn't need to look at Austin to know the square shape of his jaw. The happy glint in his sky blue eyes as he fed the chickens. The smattering of freckles across the bridge of his nose.

He'd grown out a beard in the last few months, which had taken his baby face into a man's features—and something Shay could barely resist.

Austin preferred a dark cowboy hat, as Shay had never seen him wear anything but black, or brown, or dark gray. She'd grown up with her own cowgirl hat preferences, so she understood. She wasn't obsessed with Austin or anything.

Certainly not.

Just because he was the only man in the past decade to stir something inside her that hadn't so much as been disturbed since her high school boyfriend didn't mean she noticed what kind of shirts he wore, or that his boots weren't from any shop in town, or that he had a specific type of Texan drawl that made Shay shiver whenever he spoke.

Shawna took the group through a class on a strategy to deal with anger when it came on suddenly, like it did when she got bumped into by a handsome man and something spilled on the both of them.

She used her excellent peripheral vision to look at his shirt. It still looked wet to her, and as hers still was, she could only assume it was cold and sticky as well. She wanted to cross her arms over the stain to keep her emotions from leaking out, the way she'd done at that blasted wedding where he'd asked her to dance.

He'd been drop-dead handsome in a black tuxedo, all the edges tailored and crisp. He used a cologne or an aftershave with cedar and musk in it, and the scent called to her like catnip to a feline.

It had taken all of her willpower to sit only a table away from him, keep her mouth shut during the songs she knew, and hurry out as soon as was socially acceptable.

Just like now.

She couldn't just make a run for it. Could she?

No. She sat inches from him, the magnetic field between them straining, while Shawna taught the lesson. When it was clear she was almost finished, Shay stood and squeezed past Austin, nearly falling into his lap.

She balanced herself with one hand against his strong shoulder, the electric current between them sharp and zipping from her fingertips to her shoulder. Yanking her hand away, she stumbled into the space between the row and the wall.

Cookies. Yes, she needed to get the cookies out. She hurried out of the room and around the corner to the small kitchen in the corner of the library. Since she liked to measure, mix, and bake when she was stressed, she had dozens of cookies in her freezer at the ranch. More than enough to bring to the anger management group every week for the next four months, probably.

She'd gotten them out of the freezer a couple of hours ago and arranged them on a tray in the kitchen here. With a quick swipe of her hand, she collected the cookies and headed back to the room where Shawna was finishing.

The librarians always made sure there was enough bottled water for the group, and Shay slid the tray next to the neat rows of bottles on the back table.

She stayed there rather than returning to that too-small seat next to that too-attractive man. Didn't matter. He seemed to be able to track her, no special equipment necessary. Wherever she sequestered herself on the ranch, he showed up with questions and seemingly genuine interest about the affairs of the ranch.

And blast it, she'd helped him. Explained all she could. Number one, it was part of her job to lend help to the owners. Number two, if she wanted to keep her job for the full twelve months she was guaranteed, she had to "be agreeable."

Seriously, that was the language in the contract. Since it was open for interpretation, Shay had done her best to be nice to Shane, Dylan, and Austin. But not too nice. Not nice enough to dance with Austin at his brother's wedding.

And while she didn't know everything about ranching, or even most of what happened at Triple Towers, she did want to keep her job there. It was comfortable at the very least, and Shay still didn't know what else to do with her life.

Shawna finished her class, and the participants clapped. Shay made her way to the front as the other woman sat down. "Thank you, Shawna," she said. "Does anyone want to share anything that happened this week and how they handled it?"

The anger management meetings weren't anything like what Shay had seen in movies or on TV. She'd hesitated attending her first one, imagining herself sitting around in a circle while she detailed how infuriating slow drivers were.

No, thank you. She didn't need to air her dirty laundry in public.

But she had come eventually, and the meetings weren't anything like what the entertainment made them to be. Shawna was a licensed therapist who taught strategies for managing stressful situations, gave homework exercises the participants could try at home during the week, and every couple of months, the meeting was just a social gathering while Shawna met with people one-on-one.

Tonight, no one raised their hand to share, and Shay felt pressure to fill the silence. But she didn't. The Army had taught her that sometimes silence was good, and sometimes it was okay to just let the quiet into your soul so you could feel and hear what you needed to feel and hear.

"All right," she finally said. "Well, I brought double chocolate chip cookies and butterscotch chip blondies. Help yourself." She gestured toward the back table and the people stood, some of them chatting with each other, some heading straight for the refreshments, and a couple quickly ducking out the back.

Austin hovered next to his chair, his eyes trained on her. She wished she didn't like it so much. At the same time, his curiosity was like a scent in the room that annoyed her to no end.

She couldn't just leave the meeting. So she employed a strategy Shawna had taught several months ago. She faced her challenge. Met it head on. Looked right into Austin's stunning blue eyes and held them with hers.

No.

The word rang in her ears as she drove out of town and back toward the ranch. She'd said it at least a half a dozen times while talking to Austin.

Is there a meeting next week?

No. That had been an easy one.

Are you in charge every week?

No. She could've elaborated for him. Explained that she was simply the person who ran the group on the second Thursday of the month. She wasn't in charge. She didn't organize anything. That was all Paula Hurdle, and she attended if she could. Tonight, though, she'd had an orchestra concert for her daughter.

Do you always bring cookies?

No. Technically, she hadn't lied. Sometimes she brought brownies or coffee cake.

Are you angry with me?

No. And really, she wasn't. She knew she wasn't. But projecting her anger onto him and his brothers was easier than carrying it on her own shoulders or placing it where it really belonged.

Did I do something wrong?

No. It wasn't his fault he had a perfectly symmetrical face, or muscles everywhere, or eyes so blue she could practically dive into them and swim around. That blame belonged to his parents.

Do you want to go grab, I don't know, a coffee or an ice cream cone?

That one had been so terribly difficult to answer. Because everything inside Shay definitely wanted to go get coffee with Austin Royal. Or ice cream. Or both.

No.

And so Shay drove down the lonely road by herself, her fingers gripping the steering wheel just a little too tightly. When she returned to her cabin, Molly and Lizzy greeted her at the door, their German shepherd tongues hanging out of their smiling mouths. "Hey, girls." She gave them both a quick pat, glad when some of her tension left her body. "Let's train, okay?"

Shay cut a piece of steak into tiny training bites and took the dogs out the back door. The light on the back porch shone far enough for her to do basic tasks, and she sent the dogs after a ball to begin with.

If she could focus on them for a while, let her spirit play with theirs, she'd calm down. Working with dogs had always been an outlet for her emotions, as had been singing.

She'd give up the singing when her mother died. Dropped out of the church choir and everything. Not that it mattered. She'd enlisted two months later and would've had to quit when she went to Basic Training anyway.

Her father had asked her to sing something for him every day once she'd come home. She'd refused every time. Singing was something she did with her mom, something she'd learned from her mom, and it simply felt wrong to do it in a world where her mom no longer was.

"Down," she told the dogs, glad her voice didn't crack with the emotion streaming through her. Some days, she barely thought of her mother. Sure, she was always there, lingering in the back of Shay's mind. But the fact that she couldn't call her didn't hurt too badly.

Other days, Shay felt like someone had dropped a piano on her chest and was pounding on the keys, sending painful reminders with every discordant note that her mother was gone.

With both dogs down, she rewarded them with a bit of steak. A truck's engine rumbled into the night air, and headlights beamed down the lane for just a moment before Austin pulled into the garage.

She couldn't see him. Her cabin was too far away for that, and it was dark besides. But somehow, her body knew he was in the near vicinity, and it wasn't happy that she'd turned him down for coffee.

Shay couldn't believe he'd asked again. She wondered how many times he'd ask to spend more time with her, and she wondered how much longer she could keep resisting him.

Did she even *want* to keep resisting him?

No.

The word flew into her mind and out of her mouth before she could even think. She was really starting to hate the word no.

CHAPTER THREE

Austin worked with Shay on Friday and Saturday, and neither of them said a word about Thursday's meeting. He passed along Shane's invitation for Thanksgiving dinner, though he'd told his brother he should invite Shay.

When Shane had given him an inquisitive look and asked why, Austin had said, "We don't get along. She won't come if I ask her."

"You work with her every day," Shane said. "And you don't get along?"

"We've worked out a system." He didn't elaborate. Shane didn't need to know that Austin was a doormat when it came to Shay. She could treat him however she wanted, and he simply took it. He hated the system, hated that there was no we when it came to establishing the system, hated that he was willing to endure her glares and her lectures simply to be with her for a few hours every day.

"Ask her," Shane had said, sealing the conversation. "I've spoken with her father. He's coming. I wouldn't be surprised if he'd already mentioned it to Shay."

Austin agreed, because that was what he always did. Nod and smile. Say yes and move on. Didn't matter if he was right or wrong.

But he knew her father hadn't mentioned it to Shay. Because Shay didn't talk to her father very often. Hardly at all, from what he'd been able to gather in the brief snippets of insight into her life she gave him.

On Saturday, as the sun sank toward the horizon, Austin started piling all the tools they'd used back into the huge tool chest in the tractor equipment shed. "So," he said. "I haven't heard if you'll come to Thanksgiving dinner. Shane wants to know who to plan for."

Shane didn't care at all. But Shay didn't need to know that.

She straightened, her tall, lithe frame athletic and feminine at the same time. Regarding Austin with a cool look that could've been considered flirty if it came from anyone but Shay, she said, "Your mother will be there, won't she?"

"Yes, ma'am."

"Is she cooking?"

Austin blinked, completely caught off-guard by the question. "I don't rightly know. She'll probably make part of dinner."

"Because I've seen what you Royal brothers eat, and we can't have cold cereal for Thanksgiving dinner."

Pure surprise flowed in Austin's veins. She'd seen what they ate? What did that mean?

"I can make a pretty awesome peanut butter and honey sandwich, I'll have you know." He grinned at her, just as shocked by that as what he'd said. He and Shay didn't talk about their lives. He wanted to, but she'd shut him down pretty fast.

Now though, something that looked strangely like a twinkle shone in her hazel eyes. "I suppose I'll come then."

Deciding to press his luck with this new vibe between them, he said, "I notice you go into church every week. I do too. Should we...maybe...do you want to ride together?" At the horrified look on her face, Austin added, "We wouldn't have to sit by each other during church or anything."

All of her shutters flew back into place, leaving her eyes emotionless and her jaw set. "I'll think about it." She wiped her hands on a blue rag and tossed it to the ground before meeting his eye with the classic laser-stare he'd grown accustomed to.

Conversation over.

Any other stupid questions, cowboy?

Austin gave her his best smile, noting that she softened slightly. At least she hadn't said no. That two-letter word seemed to be all she could say to him every other time he asked a question, so he'd take "I'll think about it," gladly.

"All right," he said. "I'm headed in. You have a good night." He left her in the equipment shed, using every ounce of willpower he had not to look back and see if she was watching him.

AUSTIN DIDN'T HEAR FROM SHAY BEFORE CHURCH, SO HE LOADED up himself and made the drive on his own. He did like the time to think, but he thought he would've liked having the sweet smell of Shay on the bench seat with him just as much.

"You've got to get over her," he lectured himself. It was clear she wasn't interested in him. Not the clean-shaven version, nor the man who wore the beard and joked about peanut butter sandwiches.

She tolerated him, and probably only because she wanted to keep her spot on the ranch until June, when her contract would expire. Shane had suggested he'd keep her on after that, but without paperwork in place, anything could happen.

He didn't see her at all at the sermon, and he wondered if maybe she'd stayed home because of him. He hoped not. The thought ate at him, gnawing all through the meeting and all the way back to the ranch. He parked outside of the garage and got out of his truck, his gaze straying down the lane to the cabins. They were smaller because of the distance, and he pulled his jacket around him, zipped it, and headed down the dirt road.

With every step, he tried to talk himself out of knocking on Shay's front door. He could go right past the cabins and to the house where Dylan lived. His brother wouldn't be there—he hated sitting around. He'd likely have taken the ATV and gone out onto the open range, the way he often did on Sundays. That, or he'd have gone into town to see Hazel.

Austin didn't want to spend the afternoon with his brothers. He had chores to do, and the work never seemed to end. But as he neared Shay's cabin, the scent of marinara sauce filled the air, and he made the deliberate decision to go up the steps and knock.

Several moments passed before she opened the door. She leaned into it and cocked her hip as she stared at him.

Austin forgot how to breathe. Her hair spilled over her shoulders, free from it's usual ponytail or braid, exposed since she wasn't wearing her normal cowgirl hat. She wore a blue T-shirt that wasn't anything special. But somehow it made her skin seem a bit more creamy, and Austin's fingers itched to touch her.

Though it was almost December, she wore a pair of cotton shorts that were probably part of her pajamas, and the temperature inside Austin reached summer proportions. And she wore glasses. He'd never seen the black frames on her face, but they somehow made her softer, sexier, than she had been previously.

"Hey," he managed to push out of his sticky throat. "You didn't go to church today?" She didn't wear much makeup to begin with, and today she wore none. She was so beautiful, it made Austin's muscles ache.

"Wasn't feeling particularly well," she said, the edge in her eyes softening.

"You wear glasses?"

"When I don't have my contacts in."

"Something smells good." He looked past her, trying to contain his raging hormones.

"Are you fishing for a lunch invitation?"

"Would you invite me to eat with you?" He crossed his arms and settled his weight on his back leg, almost a challenge.

She scanned him from his boots to the top of his hat, and when her eyes came to his again, it was the first time Austin felt like she'd sized him up and didn't find him lacking. Lightning crackled between them. Surely she felt it. He wasn't that delusional. Was he?

"What kind of dessert can you bring?" she finally asked.

Hope warred with desperation inside Austin's mind. "I could maybe ask Robin to help me make something." Then he'd have to explain a lot of things, to both Robin and Shane. But did that matter? What was he trying to hide?

His phone buzzed in his back pocket, but he ignored it. He couldn't look away from Shay, and she seemed as equally enamored with him.

"If you're just going to have someone else make it, you might as well come in and I'll help you."

Austin's eyebrows shot up. "You will? What will we make?"

"Which is your poison, cowboy? Brownies or cookies?"

Austin liked them both, but he said, "Brownies," simply because he knew he could make a batter and stick it in the oven. With cookies, he'd have to scoop and babysit them until they were all baked.

She stepped back, allowing him space to enter. "C'mon in, then. I can't be heatin' the whole ranch."

She didn't actually pay for her heat, but Austin kept that little tidbit to himself. He entered her cabin, a new excitement popping through him as he surveyed her space. It was simply furnished with a couch and loveseat in the room where he stood. The TV sat against the wall, and she had a narrow bookcase next to that. The kitchen sat at the back of the cabin, just like the one he'd lived in at Grape Seed Ranch.

A circular dining room table took up the back corner, with only two chairs. Just past the TV, a short hallway led to the two small bedrooms, with a bathroom between them. It was standard lodging for a ranch, and Austin appreciated the blue and yellow flowered curtains above the windows that lent a feminine touch. She also had a blue and green striped rug on the floor in front of the couches, with three watercolor paintings on the walls—all florals.

He stepped over to one so he wouldn't wrap her in his arms and profess his interest in her. *Baby steps*, he coached himself. She'd thought about riding into church with him. While she ultimately hadn't, did it really matter? He stood in her cabin now, and that was a huge leap forward.

"Did you paint these?" he asked when he caught the SH initials in the bottom right corner of the painting.

"Yes," she said in a curt tone.

"When?"

"In a past life." She moved into the kitchen and lifted the lid on a bubbling pot.

"Homemade?" he asked, keeping his distance. There was no way he could fit his huge frame in that tiny space with her and not touch her. He swallowed, trying to decide what to do.

"My mother's recipe." Shay glanced at him, those glasses slipping down her nose a little bit, a hint of color in her cheeks now. "She was a great cook."

Shay had never shared anything about her life, and certainly not her deceased mother. Austin nodded, somehow a silent acknowledgement that meant more than that he'd heard what she'd said. But that he understood that she was sharing with him.

"Some days just call for spaghetti and meatballs," she said, pushing her glasses back into place before bending to pull a pan out of the oven. The scent of meat mixed with the tomato and oregano, and Austin's stomach growled.

"Smells amazing," he said, taking tentative steps over to the bar. He pulled out his phone and saw that his dad had texted. He sighed, the sound obviously frustrated.

"What's wrong?" she asked, turning from the stove and facing him, the counter between them.

"It's my dad." He turned the phone so she could see it, but whipped it back to him immediately. "He has a special way of making my day worse." He could only see the first few words of the text—About Thanksgiving, I was thinking—and he didn't want to read the rest. No matter what plans had been made, no matter what had been discussed, his father always tried to manipulate the situation to his advantage.

Surprise crossed Shay's face. "I thought you got along with your dad."

Austin used to. He hadn't been able to understand why Shane had cut him off for so long, or why Dylan read the messages but didn't respond.

He did now.

He rotated the shoulder that had been injured a few years back when one of the bulls had escaped. "It's...complicated. He always tries to twist things. It took me a while to realize it." He didn't want to talk about his father, not right now, not with Shay.

"I get complicated," she said in a quite, sincere voice. She focused on the countertop and the moment between them felt tender, almost like Austin could reach across the island and touch her hand in a silent gesture of understanding.

She brightened as she looked up, gathered her hair and tossed it over her shoulder. She was magnificent when she smiled, and Austin sucked in a breath and held it.

"So, should we make the brownies while the pasta boils?" She bent to pull out another big pot, which she set in the sink and began to fill with water.

"Sure." Austin stood, too big and clumsy in this kitchen, with Shay.

"Okay, so we need eggs. Grab those from the fridge." She continued working to get the pasta ready to boil, all while instructing him to gather the ingredients they needed. "Do you want chocolate chips in the brownies? Or is that too much chocolate?"

"Is there such a thing as too much chocolate?" He moved to her side and looked down at her. She gazed up at him, and time froze. Everything inside Austin froze too. There was just Shay, just the vulnerability in her eyes behind the glasses, the playful lift of her lips.

He lifted his arm and brushed his fingers along her neck as he pushed her hair over her shoulder, the feel of her skin like silk and her hair as equally as smooth. Dozens of words crowded in his mouth, but he couldn't say any of them.

A flush filled her whole face, but she didn't move away from him, didn't move at all. Austin had the distinct feeling that something amazing was about to start, but he didn't want to jinx it. So he cleared his throat and said, "Let's add chocolate chips, yes."

CHAPTER FOUR

S hay woke on Monday with the scent of cologne and chocolate in her nose. It was heavenly, and she stayed under the covers for another few minutes, reliving the splendid afternoon she'd spent with Austin Royal the day before.

They'd talked about normal things. Nothing to do with the equipment or the ranch, and it felt so dang good to have a real friendship with someone.

She reminded herself that she had friends in town. That she didn't need to be friends with these men who'd bought her ranch out from under her. But Grape Seed Falls was far away, and it sure would be nice to have some allies out here.

So Austin happened to make her heart dance in anticipation and be the most handsome man she'd ever laid eyes on. She couldn't help that.

The brownies had come out beautifully gooey and chocolatey, and he'd seemed really proud of himself for making them. She'd turned on the TV to a sporting event to provide some background noise while they talked.

All in all, it was one of the best afternoons she'd had since returning to the ranch almost two years ago.

She'd see Austin later, and she wondered if he'd touch her again. She thought about the gentle brush of his fingers along her collarbone as she showered and dressed. She couldn't seem to *stop* thinking about the touch, which half annoyed her and half made her smile.

She had his number, but she didn't text him. He didn't message her either. They met up in the equipment shed after lunch, the way they usually did, except now her pulse pittered around in her chest. It always had in Austin's presence, but she'd been able to calm it after only a few seconds.

Now, though, she couldn't even breathe properly and her pulse remained erratic even though he worked way down on the other end from her. The hours passed, and still she felt like she needed to see a cardiologist, and quick.

When she finally decided to leave the shed and work somewhere else, he came over to her, wiping his hands on one of the blue rags they used. "Hey, so I was wondering if you'd want to go to dinner sometime."

It wasn't the first time he'd asked her out. The apprehension and hope on his face was so adorable, Shay wanted to jump into his arms and accept. Why didn't she?

She reminded herself not to play her whole hand up front. She'd had a few boyfriends during her time in the military, and it was better to go slow. Be friends. Get to know each other.

"I'm coming to dinner on Thursday," she said. "Does that count?"

"Sure, I mean, well...." Austin's eyebrows drew down into a V, and she felt bad for him. Why couldn't she admit she liked him? Why couldn't she go out with him?

Because she'd seen the way her mother's death had wrecked her father, ruined everything, and she didn't want any part of a relationship that could cause such devastation. Her mother had passed away twelve years ago, and her father had never recovered.

He'd run the ranch into bankruptcy, bought things he didn't need to fill the hole her mom had left in his life, and now lived in a small apartment in town, a far cry from the life he'd built at Triple Towers. More than that, the ranch had been in the family for four generations before him, and because he'd loved his wife so much, had been so devastated with the loss of her, he'd lost it all.

Shay would not give herself over to something that could destroy her and her life in a single moment. Oh, no. She would not. The decision had already been made—long ago—and though Austin really was a welcome addition to her life, she had more to lose than she had to gain.

His fingers touched hers, startling her out of her own mind. They were warm against hers, aligning and settling fully between hers. A sigh passed through her body, and when he said, "I want to go out with you. Just the two of us," in a sure, Texas drawl, she almost melted into a human puddle right there in the equipment shed.

"I don't know," she whispered.

He squeezed her hand. "What aren't you sure about?"

She didn't want to talk about it. "It's a long story."

Austin released her hand and fell back a step, taking the warmth of his body and the delicious smell of his cologne with him. "I've got nothing but time, Shay."

And she knew he wasn't going to go away. She didn't want him to. "I'm not telling it today."

"That's fine." He turned around and headed back to the combine he'd been working on. "Whenever you want. You tell me when you want to go out, and I'll clear my schedule."

He might as well have told her he loved her, right then and there. She didn't confirm. Couldn't. She just left the shed, hoping the big, Texas sky would help her figure out what she really wanted when it came to Austin.

SMOKE ROSE FROM THE BACKYARD OF THE HOMESTEAD, AND SHAY eyed it suspiciously, the hope of a delicious Thanksgiving dinner draining from her body. When she saw the extra four trucks in the driveway, one of which was her father's, she almost turned around and went back to her cabin.

Somehow, as if God Himself were directing her feet, she went up the steps and knocked on the front door. No one answered, but there was definite action happening behind the door, so Shay twisted the knob and entered the house where she'd grown up.

The brothers had painted all the walls the week before they'd moved in. The light blue did wonders for the age of the house, as did the new flooring they'd installed themselves. They certainly were a handy triplet, and Shay could admit she liked the light, ashy gray wood they'd put down.

A simple couch sat in the front room, with nothing else. Not even an end table. Shay supposed they didn't spend much time entertaining guests in this area of the house where her mother had always kept a vase of fresh flowers which she grew in the backyard.

Her father had lovingly cultivated the rose bushes her mother had planted along the fence the first week of their marriage. Even Shay had spent time clipping them, admiring them, and mulching them.

But not anymore, and she wondered if the brothers had done anything to winterize the bushes. Not your problem, she told herself as she took in the situation in front of her.

Austin's mother—obvious by the color of her eyes and the shape of her nose—stood at the kitchen counter, adding butter to a bowl on the stand mixer that was whipping something fierce. She glanced up when she saw Shay, but she didn't turn off the machine.

She did smile as she came around the counter and extended her hand. "Hello, dear. You must be Austin's Shay."

Austin's Shay?

Her eyebrows flew toward her hairline, but she managed to shake the older woman's hand. She smelled like cream and sugar, and Shay's heart squeezed into a too-small box inside her chest.

"Yes, ma'am," she said. "You must be his mother."

"Alex," she said. "I'm just finishing up the mashed potatoes.

Robin's got the rolls in the oven, so they'll be ready in about five minutes. And we've got stuffing right there." She indicated a foil-covered casserole pan sitting on the stovetop.

"Looks good." Shay glanced through the huge windows that looked out into the backyard. "And what's goin' on back there?" All three Royal brothers hovered around the source of the smoke, with four more ranch hands loitering nearby. Her father was obviously talking gesturing wildly with his hands.

"Oh, Shane thought he'd fry a turkey." Alex shook her head. "He's never done it before and it's not going exactly as planned."

Shay watched another plume of smoke waft from the smoker, wondering if they'd have protein at this meal or not. Robin came in from outside, her face flushed. She gave Shay a quick smile and then said, "It's okay. We'll be fine with what we've got."

Alex clucked her tongue like she was reprimanding a wayward child. "I told him we should just roast it."

"It looks great." Robin checked the rolls. "Nice and brown. The oil just keeps overflowing a little. They're trying to siphon some off. That's what's causing the smoke."

Shay looked around, noticing the empty dining room table. "Can I help? Can I set the table? Get out salt and pepper? Butter? Something?"

"Yes." Robin turned from the oven, a true grin on her face now. "I'll get everything down and you can set it up." She opened a cupboard. "Let's see...how many of us are there?" She started ticking off people—Shane, Robin, Dylan, Hazel, Austin, Shay, Alex, Shay's father, Oaker, Carlos, Dean, Chadwell, Dwayne, Felicity, Kurt, and May. "Oh, and their eighteen-month-old, Greta. And the new baby."

Sixteen people.

Shay almost fled. By sheer will and a steady stream of prayer, she took the plates Robin handed to her with half a smile. Robin came over and helped her get the double leaf out of the dining room table that was clearly an heirloom.

"Where did you guys get this table?" she asked.

"It belonged to my grandmother," Robin said. "It was the only thing I brought to the ranch that I couldn't fit in the tiny house." She glanced at Alex and then Shay. "I'm glad you came, Shay. Austin's been talkin' about you non-stop for about a week."

Since he showed up at the anger management meeting. She still wasn't sure why he'd come. She'd never sensed any fury in him before, though he'd revealed a few things about his father that surely caused him some frustration and annoyance.

"Oh yeah?" Shay finished with the leaf while Robin returned to the rolls as the timer shrilled through the kitchen.

Alex got out the silverware and glasses, and Shay matched them as best as she could, making each place setting unique. She added two plates of butter, two sets of salt and pepper shakers, as well as a little bowl of gravy and two jars of peach jam.

Alex and Robin lined up the food on the countertop, buffet style, and as one, all three women looked out the window. The smoke had cleared at least.

"Looks like a maybe," Alex said.

"I'll go check on them," Robin said. "You want to come with me, Shay?"

Before she could answer or follow Robin, Shane lifted the turkey from the fryer, the bird beautifully golden brown. The doorbell rang, and Shay turned that way too.

"I'll get it," she said when Robin continued outside and Alex kept basting the rolls with butter.

Four people—two couples—and two kids waited on the front porch. Shay recognized Dwayne Carver, and got introduced to his foreman, Kurt, his wife, May, and their two kids, Greta and Phillip.

Dwayne's wife introduced herself as Felicity as everyone herded into the house, the little girl calling for Dylan like they were old pals.

"Dinner's on," Shane called in a loud voice, silencing a lot of the chatter as everyone piled into the kitchen and dining room. Shay joined everyone, staying on the fringes, skirting her gaze away from Austin though he refused to look anywhere but at her.

"We're so glad you could all join us here at the ranch," Shane said, swallowing as his pale blue eyes turned glassy and bright. The silence that followed was emotionally charged as all of the brothers looked around at their guests.

"It's our first holiday here," Dylan said. "And we're glad we have each other and all of you with us." He looked at Austin, elbowing him when the youngest brother still stared at Shay.

"Yeah," Austin said. "Hopefully, this is the first of a lot of Thanksgiving dinners at Triple Towers."

"With less smoke," Robin said, laughing. Everyone laughed, and Shay allowed herself to relax a little. The atmosphere in the homestead was familial, comfortable, wonderful. Shay wanted this feeling all the time. The happiness and joy she'd had when her mother made mashed potatoes and her father carved the turkey.

She was sure that would never exist again in this place, but here she stood, basking in it. These three men had brought it with them. Their family. Their friends and ranch hands. And Shay wanted to be part of it. That craving had never gone away, though she'd gone away from Triple Towers.

"Let's say grace," Alex said, and Shane asked Kurt to say the prayer. It was a beautiful prayer that further soothed Shay's soul, and when he finished, she moved over to say hello to her father. She'd been so, so angry at him when she'd returned from her time in the Army.

He'd let the ranch fall into ruin. He'd spent every penny he had, and a whole lot he didn't have. He'd piled the huge, five-thousand square-foot homestead with things he'd bought. Most of them were unopened, with tags and shipping receipts still in the boxes. His hoarding had caused the bathroom behind the kitchen to be unuseable, and Shay had spent the better part of a month working on the plumbing and installing a new toilet, tub-shower combo, and tile before they could list the ranch for sale.

Not that they'd ever listed it. Her dad had gone to Dwayne, something Shay had suggested. She knew Dwayne, thought maybe he'd buy the place and let her run it. She hadn't counted on him offering the ranch to the Royal brothers.

She swallowed back the bitterness, the gratitude of this day overwhelming those negative emotions. "Hey, Daddy," she said.

His face brightened, and he gave her a side hug. "How goes it, Shayleigh?"

"Just fine." She glanced around the room, the others gathering plates from the table and forming a line to move down the bar and collect all the Thanksgiving wares.

"It's good to see you," he said, and while Shay knew he didn't mean to imply that she was a bad daughter for not stopping by more often, that was still how she felt.

"What are you doing to stay busy?" she asked her father. She paid all his bills and had taken away all his credit and debit cards. She'd sold everything she could in an attempt to pay off his debt, and with the sale of the ranch, he'd come out clean and higher than he'd been. So she gave him a monthly allowance for groceries, in cash, and she paid everything else.

"Playing chess," he said. "The community center hosts it every Tuesday, Wednesday, and Thursday."

Shay looked at him in surprise. "That's great, Daddy."

"The ranch looks good." His tone carried a note of casualness that Shay knew was false. Her father had loved this ranch. When she'd come home to find it broken down, bankrupt, and her father a shell of who she'd left a decade earlier, the only option had been to sell the place.

He'd fought her every step of the way, until finally his best friend and fellow rancher, Chase Carver, had come out and given him the same assessment she had. Her dad blamed her for the loss of Triple Towers; she blamed him.

In general, he was a big reason she went to anger management classes every Thursday.

"You look good, Shay." He peered at her, the age that sometimes clouded his eyes clearing. "Things must be going well here."

Shay allowed herself a glance in Austin's direction. He was

moving through the line behind his mother, chatting with her in an easy, casual way. "Yeah," she said. "Things are going well here."

An hour later, fully satiated with turkey, mashed potatoes, gravy, and cranberry sauce—and rolls and jam. Oh, the rolls and peach jam!—Shay leaned away from the table as the conversation continued around her.

She felt sleepy, but she didn't want to leave this comfortable place. Austin sat four spots away from her, easy to look at, and her gaze had drifted in his direction several times during the meal.

Someone mentioned Christmas, and what the brothers would be doing, and her father said, "This ranch used to be the place to be in December."

The conversations hushed, and Shane said, "What do you mean?"

"We used to put up hundreds, no, thousands, of lights," he said. "On all the towers. Santa on the roof. Everything you can think of. People would come out and drive through." He smiled as he obviously relived the happier memories in his own mind.

"Right, Shay?" He looked at her. "Dwayne?"

"I do remember that," Dwayne said. "We could see the lights all the way down at our homestead." He flashed a friendly grin. "Why'd you stop doing it?"

Shay pulled in a breath and watched her father. What would he say? Should she jump in?

"Oh, you know." He chuckled, but Shay heard all the unspoken reasons. "Life got busy."

No, her mother had died. Shay pressed her lips together, only releasing them when Austin caught her eye and lifted his brows.

"What did you do with all the lights?" Shane asked. "I don't think we saw anything like that lying around." He looked at Dylan, who shook his head. Austin likewise shrugged his shoulders.

But Shay knew where it all was. After all, she was the one tasked with cleaning up a decade of her father's mess. She was the one who'd taken charge, made the decisions her dad seemed incapable of making, and had decided what to keep and what to throw away.

The lights, the decorations, the huge star they put on the tall water tower every year? Her mother had adored them. Shay had loved them. And she simply hadn't been able to throw the decorations away, though they were in dire need of cleaning and repair. Some should probably be replaced, and a twinge of hope that the ranch could be as glorious this Christmas as it once had been was too much to keep her silent.

"I know where they are," she said.

Every eye at the table swung toward her, and Shay hated carrying the weight of all of them. Sure, she was used to people staring at her. It seemed that a female Army mechanic was curious to some people, as was a five-foot-ten-inch woman who chose to wear four-inch heels.

"You do?" her father asked.

"I kept them," she said. "They're in the storage shed out by the silos."

Shane looked like he was thinking really hard, the lines around his eyes creasing. Dylan didn't seem to care at all, but Austin was watching her with a glint in those gorgeous eyes that spelled trouble for Shay.

And not the kind she'd gotten into with the ranch hands growing up. Not sneaking out to go horseback riding by moonlight. But the kind that would break her heart.

And when he said, "I'd like to see them," she knew they'd be spending a lot more time together, whether she liked it or not.

CHAPTER FIVE

Austin stood outside the small storage shed between the four silos. The morning air was crisp, almost stinging his lungs—at least for Texas. He'd seen this building before and just assumed it held the mechanics for the silos. But standing in front of it now, he could see it stretched back farther than he'd thought and could certainly house a ranch's worth of Christmas decorations.

After the conversation had moved to other things on Thanksgiving, and pie had been served, and some people had taken their coffee into the living room, Austin had found Jack Hatch and asked him to see pictures of the ranch when it was decorated for Christmas.

The thrill of it still shone in his mind's eye, and Austin really wanted to bring that magic back to Triple Towers this year. He could feed the chickens and keep up with the machinery and put up a few lights.

He tried the knob of the door of the shed, but it didn't budge. So Shay had the key. She hadn't looked super thrilled yesterday afternoon when he'd said he wanted to see the lights, but she couldn't keep him out of this shed.

He owned it now. He could change the locks without telling her if he wanted to. But he didn't want to. Just like he had this insatiable need to take her to dinner, he craved making this ranch as wonderful and as happy as it had once been for her.

As his hometown ranch had been for him. He *had* to create a place like that. For himself. For his future family. For Shay.

Why, he wasn't sure. It was simply something that drove him.

His phone rang, and he swiped it on without checking who the caller was. A mistake he couldn't take back when he heard his father's voice.

"Austin," he boomed as if they were old pals.

Austin turned away from the locked storage shed full of possibilities. "Dad."

"I never heard from you about Thanksgiving. I'm assuming you spent it with your mother on the ranch."

He pushed out a sigh, hoping the frustration would carry through the line. "You know we did, Dad. I communicated the plan to you." And he didn't appreciate his father trying to change it last-minute. But he didn't say that. He never did.

"Well, Joanna and I would like to host Christmas at our place."

"Shane and Dylan won't come," Austin said automatically. He didn't want to go either. "We've already got plans for the ranch." He turned back to the shed, his mind sifting through what could be inside. Stars. Candy canes. Reindeer.

"You boys are always welcome here," his dad said. "Always. I've never said you couldn't come."

Not in words. It had taken Austin years to understand that actions spoke louder than words.

"Will you mention it to Shane and Dylan, at least?" His father had always put Austin up to tasks like these. Austin had spent the better part of a decade conflicted, torn between his brothers who had taken care of him, and his loyalty to his father.

Today, he was tired of the game. Tired of being played. His anger started as an ember deep in his gut, but it accelerated quickly. "No, Dad," he said, deciding to use the tactic that therapist had taught at the anger management class. Face the conflict head-on.

"No?" His dad seemed genuinely confused.

"No, Dad," Austin repeated. "I'm not going to talk to Shane or Dylan about coming for Christmas. It's our first season on the ranch, and we want to establish our own traditions."

The silence on the other end of the line unsettled Austin. "Hey," he said. "I have to go. I'll talk to you later." He hung up before his dad could find another way to manipulate him. Before the anger could escalate into fury. Before he got sucked into his father's games again.

He tried the doorknob one more time. Still locked. Annoyance sang through him as he turned away. He needed a key. So he'd go get a key.

Shay wasn't home, or at least she wasn't answering the door when he pounded on it.

Reminding himself that he didn't need to go breaking down her door, he stepped back, his breath coming faster than he would've liked.

His frustration almost felt like a being all its own, and he hated the darkness it filled him with. He hurried down Shay's steps and back to the dirt lane running in front of the cabins. He walked away from the crossroads, passing all the other cabins, then Dylan's house, and on down the road until it ended at a T-junction, one road leading north and one south along the edge of a hay field.

He could literally wander this ranch for days and not touch the same spot of ground twice. He loved Texas, the wild land, the ability to raise cattle, and ride horses, and listen to the wind tell secrets to the trees.

He breathed, finding a way through his anger until he could calm himself down. Thinking more rationally, he pulled out his phone and sent a text to Shay. *Would you mind if I looked through the Christmas décor?*

She didn't answer right away, and he wondered where she was.

Her truck hadn't been in front of her cabin, which probably should've been his first clue that she wouldn't answer the door.

He'd settled enough and had started back toward the epicenter of the ranch when his phone chimed.

I ran into town to see a friend this morning, Shay had said. *I'll be back this afternoon and we can go through the shed together, if that's okay.*

Of course it was okay. Austin didn't want to say exactly that though, in case he came across as too eager.

"Can't come across any stronger," he muttered to himself. He'd held her hand in the equipment shed. Asked her out—again. Told her right to her face—with his perfectly serious—that he wanted dinner alone with her.

He wasn't blind. He'd seen the spark of interest in her eyes the first time they'd met. She'd let him hold her hand, and her fingers had curled around his too. Yes, Shay liked him just fine, no matter how much she'd bossed him or argued with him.

There was something making her pull back, shut down, close off from him. And the further she retreated, the more he wanted to chase her down and make her talk to him.

Just text me when you get back, he typed out and sent. Then he headed over to the chicken coops, hoping time with the cluckers would relax him.

SHAY MET HIM AT THE STORAGE SHED, AND AUSTIN COULDN'T help the way his smile spread across his face. Her glasses were gone, and her long, thick hair had been pulled up high on her head again. She wore a dark wash pair of jeans with a sweatshirt that had a silhouette of a German shepherd on it, and her two dogs trotted at her side.

"Hey, girls." Austin crouched down and extended his hand to the dogs.

"Sit," Shay commanded, and both dogs complied instantly.

They were beautiful animals, clearly loyal to Shay, with their long tongues hanging out of their mouths. They both looked at Austin for a few seconds, then the bigger one looked back at Shay, as if asking her permission.

"Lizzy, go."

The big dog came forward, her nose sniff, sniff, sniffing, and Austin chuckled as he scrubbed her behind the ears.

"Molly," Shay said in a warning tone. Finally, the other German shepherd turned her head and looked at Shay.

"Go."

Molly jetted forward too, practically knocking Lizzy out of the way. "Are they sisters?" he asked.

"Yes," Shay said. "Molly's the runt, and Lizzy was the pack leader. She barked a lot when she was a pup, and no one wanted her."

Austin glanced up, hearing something dangerous behind Shay's words. "You wanted her."

"She's an excellent dog." Shay loosened up slightly, dropping her arms from how she had them clenched across her middle. "And she doesn't bark anymore."

"I've never heard her." Lizzy licked his face, and he laughed and pushed her away.

"They like you." Shay sounded surprised, and Austin straightened.

"I think they like everyone," he said, facing the shed.

"Not really." She stepped over to the door and fitted a key into the lock. She hesitated before twisting it, her eyes reaching up to find his.

"What?" he asked, his voice turning tender though he had no idea how he'd made it do that.

"This is...personal to me," she said. "I know you own it, and that's fine and all, but this is—these decorations mean a lot to me." Shay looked raw, filled with so much emotion, so many memories, so much to her past that Austin really wanted to know.

He cupped her cheek in one palm and said, "All right. Let's take a look."

She leaned into his touch, her eyes drifting closed. In that moment, Austin could see how she'd look just before he'd kiss her. Oh, how he wanted to kiss her. And now she'd given him the perfect visual, which would haunt him in the time it took him to fall asleep from now until forever.

Austin leaned toward her, almost mindlessly. Then she opened her eyes, he snapped to attention, and she twisted the key to open the door.

"Some of it might be in disrepair," she said, pushing the door in and stepping after it.

He followed her into the shed. "Tell me more about the light show." Austin could feel the dust against his fingertips already, and he hadn't even touched anything yet.

Shelves lined both walls of the shed, leading all the way to the back, where a set of double doors revealed a cabinet. Shay pulled a string hanging from the ceiling and a bare light bulb blazed to life.

Boxes and bins sat on the shelves, some with labels and some without. Two toolboxes sat on the floor just inside the door, and Austin brushed the tip of his boot against one of them. The bottom points of a gigantic star poked out from the bottom shelf, and he pulled it out.

"Where did this go?"

Shay looked at him, the nostalgia written all over her face. "The water tower. It lights up. My grandfather hung it for years until my dad took over." She traced her fingertips down the point closest to her.

"So we put lights on everything. The fences, the posts, the stables, the house, all the cabins, every tree trunk and branches. It was beautiful. Magical. In the last few years before I left, my mom programmed the lights to go with music, and people could tune their radios to a specific station and listen along with the lights."

She sighed, pulling her hand back. Austin slid the star back onto the shelf and reached for a box marked "red and white lights." He pulled it down while she continued.

"We'd put those around the silos to make candy canes," she said. "The star on the tallest tower. Icicle lights on all the sheds." She extracted a trio of circles from a low shelf. "These are snowmen. They have hats somewhere."

The more she talked and the more Austin looked at, the more he wanted to get this all set up. Pull it all out. Test it all. Fix what had burnt out. And spend the next week or two transforming this ranch into that magical place Shay spoke of.

If not for her, for him. He could really use some magic in his life right now, though if he could get Shay to go out with him, that alone would give him a high that would take a long time to come down from.

Instead of asking, he started pulling out more bins and boxes and taking them outside. He sorted them into piles of lights— blue, white, red, and multi-colored. She brought out the snowmen, and he counted eight of them. The star got it's own spot. The icicle lights kept coming and coming, as did the eight not-so-tiny reindeer and the plywood that was in need a fresh coat of red paint in order to be Santa's sleigh.

He found more shapes like the snowmen, but they weren't round. Various rectangles in various sizes. "What are these?" he asked, tilting them toward Shay, who was crouched at the back of the shed, looking through something.

She twisted to look over her shoulder. "Soldiers. Toy soldiers."

"Ah, of course." He could see the legs, the bodies, the boxy hats now that he knew what he was looking for.

She straightened and held up a series of circles. "And these expand to Christmas trees. We have them in blue, white, red, green, purple, and pink."

"How many?"

"Probably four dozen. My mother loved them."

Austin smiled at her. "You loved your mother."

She flinched the teensiest bit before bending to pick up the box. She passed it to him, holding onto it while he did too. Their eyes met under the glow of that light bulb, and she nodded. "I loved my mother. I miss her so much." She swallowed once, and then again. "Some days, I'm fine. But this? Going through all of this stuff she loved?" She shook her head and sighed. "I miss her."

Austin's heart bled for her. "I'm so sorry, Shay."

She released the box. "I think we should do it. See what works and get it all up. My mother would've loved it, and I think it's just what this ranch needs right now."

"Really?" Austin couldn't help the hope in his voice. He'd been planning to ask her if he could please put up the decorations, and now he didn't have to.

She smiled and bumped him to get him to go out of the shed. "Really."

He chuckled and walked backward until he made it into the sunshine, moving past all the other boxes to start a new pile for the four dozen trees they needed to bring out from the shed.

CHAPTER SIX

Shay paced in her cabin, her heels making her more anxious than she already was. If she didn't text Austin in the next five minutes, he'd leave for church without her. She knew. She'd tracked his schedule for months.

"Don't you ever tell him that," she told herself, gripping her phone too tightly and making another pass toward the front door and back. Of course she wouldn't tell him. So she was detail-oriented and extremely observant. Both skills had served her well in the Army, but sometimes they became a bit of a shock for the average person.

"Just do it," she muttered to herself, making her thumbs fly across the touch keyboard and send the message she'd wanted to send last week.

With it done, her nerves deflated and she sank onto the couch. Now all she do was wait, and she didn't like it. Was this how Austin felt when he asked her out and she just stared back at him? The poor guy. And he'd done it more than once, which really testified of his character—and his interest in her.

Sure, he messaged back. *I'm just leaving now. I'll come pick you up.*

Only a minute later, the sound of his truck rumbled to a stop in front of her cabin. Shay jumped to her feet and hurried around the couch so she could meet him before he came all the way to her front door.

After all, it was just church. Not a date. They wouldn't even sit by one another once they arrived in town. Shay would make sure of that.

Just because they'd spent a day and a half unloading the Christmas decorations, sorting them, and testing them didn't mean she was ready to open herself to the possibility of love. She didn't want the most exciting part of her future to be chess on Tuesdays, Wednesdays, and Thursdays. And she would not let her entire life be ruined when the love of her life was lost.

She held onto the railing as she moved down the steps and onto the gravel. With her tall black heels, she didn't need to face plant in front of the cowboy she was crushing on. She tugged on the hem of her dress—pure black from shoulder to knee—her nerves getting the best of her in the worst moment possible.

When she finally lifted her gaze to Austin, she found him to be a vision straight out of a Hollywood western, wearing black slacks that seemed tailored exactly for him. His white shirt practically glowed in the weak winter sunlight, and the bright blue tie rivaled his eyes in brilliance. And the dark gray cowboy hat undid her composure completely.

"Hey, beautiful," he said in that smooth, bass voice of his, and she wanted to hear him call her beautiful every day of her life. Maybe they could be the type of friends that kissed sometimes. Held hands as they walked toward his truck, as they were right now.

She sure enjoyed the heat and weight of his hand along her back as he held open her door for her and helped her into the truck. Settling her skirt to cover her legs properly, she gave him a smile. Friends could smile at each other.

She watched him walk around the front of the truck, his mouth in a shape indicating his whistle, wondering when she'd even started seeing him as a friend. He'd been a man she tolerated.

A man who'd bought *her* ranch. A man who'd lit something in her that hadn't been near fire in years.

He ceased whistling when he got in the truck, and he started it up and pulled out in silence. After fiddling with the radio, he started to hum along, seemingly at complete ease with her. Shay was grateful he wasn't all keyed up, because she certainly was.

"I haven't told my brothers about the anger management," he said when they pulled from the dirt road of the ranch and onto the asphalt of the road leading to town. He cut her a glance out of the side of his eye. "And I want to keep it that way."

"All right," she said. "I wouldn't have told them."

"I didn't think you would," he said. "I just didn't want it to slip or something."

She turned toward him slightly. "What are you going to tell them? Where do they think you're going on Thursday nights?"

He shifted on the seat, a slight cough escaping his mouth. "Bible study class."

Shay blinked, the irony of the situation bubbling out of her mouth. "Bible study class," she repeated around her giggles. "So you're lying about going to church. Seems a bit off, don't you think?"

Austin shrugged, but a smile definitely pulled at the corners of his mouth too. "I suppose." He removed his right hand from the wheel and extended it toward her, a very clear invitation for her to slide across the seat and sit beside him, the way girlfriends rode in trucks with their boyfriends.

Shay hesitated for a split second, and then she did what felt natural to her: She slid across the seat and took his hand in hers.

"Have you thought any more about dinner?" he asked.

"Yes." Her voice came out as a whisper. Did he know he'd been torturing her for a week because of that invitation?

"And?" He looked at her, the road in front of them deserted. He'd probably driven it a thousand times anyway.

"I'm still thinkin' about it."

Austin stiffened, an almost imperceptible movement, but Shay felt it in the length of his leg that was closest to hers. "What about church, then? We can sit by each other at church maybe."

"Yeah, sure," she said, even though only ten minutes ago she'd told herself that she would definitely not be sitting by him at church.

"Shane said we could have the money to fix up the decorations and get the additional ones we need."

Joy filled her at the very idea that Triple Towers Ranch would be lit up for the holidays again. "That's great."

"He said we have to work on it on our own time," he said. "We can't fall behind in our other work."

"Of course," Shay said. "Believe it or not, I used to keep up with all of this stuff before you guys came along."

Austin flinched as if she'd punched him, and regret filled her. He pulled his hand away and put it on the steering wheel with the words, "I know that. I wasn't saying—a"

"I'm sorry," she blurted out. "I'm...sometimes I—a" She looked at him, searching his face for any hint of how he felt. He wouldn't look at her, and she supposed he shouldn't what with him driving and all.

"I think I understand," he said, his jaw twitching with how tight he held it. "You don't like me or my brothers because we bought your ranch." He glanced her way. "Am I close?"

She folded her hands into her lap. "Sort of."

A half a mile went by before he said, "Tell me about it."

And because he spoke in such a calming voice, and his fingers weren't quite so tight on the wheel anymore, Shay breathed in deep and tried to calm her frantically beating heart. This time, it wasn't jumping around because of his nearness. Or because of his tantalizing cologne. But because it was absolutely terrified she might have driven him away when she wanted to bring him closer.

Another deep breath, and she started. "By the time you saw the homestead, I'd hauled out ninety percent of what my father had filled it with."

Austin jerked his attention to her. "Really?"

"He's a hoarder," she said simply. "It started after my mother passed away, and after I—" Her voice stuck in her throat.

Ran away.

That was what her father would say.

"Left for the Army," was what Shay allowed herself to say. She stared out the windshield, the countryside blurring by as looked at it unfocused. "He spent every dime we had. Then more. It took me six months to go through the stuff in the house, sell it all, and get the place ready to sell. Six months."

It was six months she never wanted to experience again. Didn't want to think about or remember those days.

Austin slipped his fingers between hers again. "When did you start anger management?"

"A few weeks after I got back and saw what my father had done with the ranch." The words flowed from her easily, and she realized that she trusted Austin.

In her world, she'd only trusted herself and those in her unit. They had her back, her very life if necessary. And she'd done the same for them. Just like her mother, she missed her unit in the Army from time to time. Perhaps not quite as deeply, and not quite as strongly, but she missed them nonetheless.

Her life had taken on a dreariness since she'd retired, with only her father to look after—and he didn't even seem to know he needed looking after.

"I started because of my father too," Austin said, a troubled note in his voice.

"Where is he?"

"He lives in San Antonio. We had a ranch just north of the city. I grew up there. Shane was set to take it over; it had been in our family for generations, like your ranch." He spoke in a monotone now, almost like he'd removed himself from this painful part of his past. Shay didn't like it, wanted the emotional, animated version of Austin to return.

"He did a bunch of stuff I didn't really get at the time. I was only sixteen. What I remember is Shane and my mom talking a lot, behind closed doors. Then they sold the ranch, and my mom moved into a condo, and Shane took me and Dylan to work at a new ranch." He looked at her, softening a little.

"Your ranch is a brand new start for us. Something we hope we can pass down through our families."

Shay nodded, her emotion too much and flowing too fast for her to conceal it should she speak.

"He's...he texts me the most. For a long time, I didn't understand why my brothers didn't like him. But he keeps...manipulating me. And it makes me really angry." His fingers tightened against hers, and she squeezed back, about all she could do at the moment.

Austin fell silent after that, clearly wrapped up in his own memories, his own past. Shay let him go, because she needed the silence this drive provided, and she was glad he gave it to her, only the low warbling of the radio in the background.

By the time they arrived at the church, Shay had sorted through a few things and made one big decision. She put her hand on Austin's arm as he started to get out of the truck.

He looked at her, right into her eyes, all the way past all of her defenses. "I'd like to go to dinner with you," she said.

A smile burst onto his face, and he said, "Yeah?"

She grinned too, glad to be knocking down some of her walls. "Yeah."

CHAPTER SEVEN

A ustin blinked at Dylan and then Shane. "She has what?"
"A boyfriend," Dylan said.
"*Our* mom?"

"Yes," Shane said, sitting at the bar with a cup of coffee. "She's bringing him for Christmas." He returned to the notebook that he carried everywhere with him. It contained everything about the ranch, and he studied it, added notes to it, and stapled things inside constantly.

Austin wasn't sure how to feel. "How long have they been dating?"

"Six months." Shane scratched out another sentence and turned the page. "She didn't say anything at Thanksgiving, because she wanted it to be about us and the ranch."

Of course she did. Austin knew his mother to be the most self-less person on the planet. Still, he couldn't quite imagine her holding hands with a man, or wanting to go through another relationship when her first marriage had ended so disastrously.

"What's his name?"

"Brian?" Dylan guessed, pulling open the fridge and pulling out the milk. A carton of cream joined it, and Austin gestured that he wanted Rice Krispies with cream too.

"No, it's Barry," Shane said without looking up.

"Is it?" Dylan got down two bowls with a shrug. "It starts with a B, I know that."

Austin wanted to tell them about his date with a woman whose name started with an S, but he didn't quite know how. He had to say something to get the truck and get off the ranch that night. Unless Shay could drive....

Dylan slid him a bowl overflowing with Rice Krispies, and Austin started pouring cream and then milk on them, enjoying the way they talked back to him. "So, I'm going into town tonight." He cleared his throat, hoping maybe that would do it. Be enough. No explanation needed. "Can I take the truck?"

"I'm using it," Dylan said. "Hazel and I are going to the Christmas Spectacular at Sunshine Farms, remember?" He spoke of his fiancée with ease, and Austin wondered if he'd ever be able to do the same with Shay.

"We need another vehicle," Austin said, frowning into his cereal.

"What do you need it for?" Shane asked. "You could ask Robin to borrow hers."

Robin had a nice truck that cost more than Austin even wanted to think about. His face heated and he stuffed his mouth full of the popping cereal to give himself a few seconds to think.

Might as well tell them...they're going to find out soon enough.

He swallowed. "I, uh, well, I have a date."

Shane finally lifted his eyes from the notebook and Dylan let his milk drip, drip, drip back into his bowl, his spoon frozen in mid-air.

"A date?" Dylan asked. "With who? You haven't been off the ranch in months."

"I go to church every week," Austin said. Seriously, was him going out with someone that big of a deal? "So yeah, maybe Robin would let me borrow your truck? I'll ask her." He looked at Shane and shoved another huge bite of cereal into his mouth, suddenly keen to finish eating and get out of the kitchen.

"She's already out on a job," Shane said. "You can text her."

Austin reached for his phone, but Shane was faster. He swiped it from its spot on the counter between them. "*After* you tell me who you're goin' out with."

"Come on." Austin rolled his eyes. "I go out with plenty of women."

Shane and Dylan exchanged a glance. "Not for about a year, I believe," Shane said.

"You're keeping track?"

"Someone has to."

Austin huffed out his annoyance. "I'm not a baby," he said. "I'm thirty-three, and I can go out with whoever I want."

"You sure can," Dylan said with a wicked grin. "We just want to know who she is."

"Was I this annoying when you started dating Hazel?"

"Yes," Dylan said. "You both were, if you'll recall." He gave his brothers pointed looks, and Austin couldn't really argue with him.

"You have to promise not to be weird about it," Austin said, like that would help at all. Shane and Dylan would tease him mercilessly, just as they had with every girlfriend he'd ever had.

Girlfriend.

The word felt half-right and half-wrong in his mind. Shay wasn't his girlfriend—not yet.

"Why would we be weird?" Shane asked. "I'll be happy for you. Hopefully it'll work out." He sounded sincere, and Austin saw the genuineness in his eyes too.

"All right." He drew in a deep breath. "It's Shay."

Silence cloaked the kitchen. Dylan finally said, "Shay, as in the woman who dislikes us because we bought her ranch out from underneath her?"

"Did she tell you that?" Austin asked.

"It's obvious," Dylan said. He narrowed his eyes and peered at Austin like he could see through bone and skin to his brain beneath. "What have you two been doing in the equipment shed all these months?"

"Working," Austin said quickly, glancing at Shane and looking away. "Talking." That heat filled his whole body now, and he was sure he was flushing. "I asked her to dance at your wedding. She refused."

"How many times have you asked her out?" Shane asked, his voice barely above a whisper.

"I don't know," Austin said. "Four maybe."

Shane stood and drained the last of his coffee. "Hey, at least it didn't take you three years to get her to say yes." He flashed Austin a smile and said, "You can take Robin's truck. I'll text her." He set the phone down beside Austin and headed out the back door to get to work.

Dylan finished his cereal in silence, and Austin was glad for it. Just when he sensed Dylan was about to head out too, Austin asked, "I'm not making a mistake, am I?"

"Why would you think that?"

"Well, she works here. What if I screw things up and it makes life difficult for all of us?"

"She's definitely been prickly," Dylan said. "But if she said yes to a date with you, you must be doin' something right." He put his bowl in the sink. "Don't worry so much about it. Go with your gut." And with that, he left Austin alone in the homestead, wondering if his gut wanted more cereal or if it was telling him to get out to the silos so he and Shay could start decorating the ranch for Christmas.

SHAY SHOWED UP ON THE FRONT PORCH OF THE HOMESTEAD instead of allowing Austin the chance to collect her from her cabin.

"Hey," he said, sitting next to her on the top step. "You could've come in."

"I was early." She tucked her hair behind her ear. She wore it down again tonight, the blonde streaks catching the winter sunlight and reflecting them. Her smile revealed straight, white teeth and a happy glow about her that Austin had rarely seen.

They'd worked in the equipment shed for only an hour that afternoon, then she'd gone out to mow a field somewhere. She'd showered, obviously, and she wore her glasses again tonight.

He reached out and touched them. "No contacts?"

"I got some hay or something in my eye this afternoon. It hurts." She carefully wiped her forefinger beneath her right eye.

Sure enough, it looked redder than the other one. "Is it okay?"

"Feeling better now," she said. "But I didn't want to wear my contacts." She hugged her knees, bunching up the floral fabric of her skirt. "I'm dressed okay?"

Austin's throat felt like sand. "Yeah, of course." He wore jeans and a black polo under a leather jacket. She looked bright, beautiful, and fun while he could be riding a motorcycle to a bar.

"Am I dressed okay?" he teased, wondering what she thought of the cowboy-biker look.

She grinned as she ran two fingertips along the brim of his cowboy hat. "This would be better in black, with this particular look."

Austin stood, reaching down to take her hand and help her to her feet too. "I have black."

"I know. I saw it at the wedding." Her eyes glinted like gems, and Austin worked hard not to lean down and kiss her before they'd even gone out.

His mother had counseled him never to kiss a woman on the first date, but Dylan had kissed Hazel *before* they'd even gone out. Of course, they had spent several days together out in a cabin, so Austin assumed they'd talked plenty before the actual kissing.

"Should I go grab it?"

She shrugged. "Sure. If you want."

He wanted to be who she wanted, so he said, "Give me a minute." He took her in the house with him and left her in the

living room with the single couch while he took the steps leading
upstairs two at a time.

He knew right where the hat was, and he pulled it out of the
box in the top of his closet, his heart thrumming a steady pulse in
his neck. "Calm down," he told himself. But it was hard to find
that inner peace. He'd been dreaming of a date, of dinner, of dancing, with Shay for six months. Okay, only five. It was still a long
time, and he was sure he was going to go back downstairs and find
she'd fled.

With that panicked thought in his mind, he practically
sprinted back to the living room to find her sitting on the couch,
studying her fingernails. "Ready?" he asked.

She stood, the nerves in her expression not quite evaporating
before she met his eyes. "Yeah. Ready."

Austin laced his fingers through hers deliberately, enjoying
every thrill and spark at the way her hand fit in his. "I'm glad you
said yes," he said, not trying to make his voice sound like he'd swallowed cotton. "Do you have a favorite place in town?"

"Yeah." She hesitated. "You won't like it."

Austin led her toward the front door and outside. "Why do you
say that?"

"Most men don't."

"I'm sure it'll be fine."

"Every time I go there, it's all women eating with their kids or
girlfriends." She paused as he opened her door and stood back so
she could climb in Robin's high-end truck. "You'll definitely
stand out."

"I'm with you," he said. "Of course I'll stand out." He gave her
a smile that felt flirty on his face, and her blush confirmed it. "And
a place without other men to steal you away from me sounds great.
What's this place called?"

"The Soup Kitchen." She watched him for a reaction, but
Austin couldn't give her one.

"Never been there."

"The whole menu is soup. I love soup."

"Soup it is, beautiful." Austin helped her into the truck and closed the door before heading around the back. Truth was, soup wasn't his favorite food. But he didn't care. Not even a little bit. He'd eat cardboard if it meant Shay was sitting across the table from him, that gorgeous hair cascading around her beautiful face and shoulders, telling him things about herself he didn't yet know.

In fact, as soon as he buckled his seat belt and got his bearings in this unfamiliar vehicle, he said, "Tell me something about yourself I don't know." He put the truck in reverse and backed away from the garage before setting the truck toward the main road. He'd bumped the minute or two down the dirt lane before he realized Shay hadn't said a word.

He stopped before turning and looked at her. "Shay?"

"I'm trying to think of something."

He chuckled, a bit of nervous energy entering the cab. "I don't know hardly anything about you," he said. "It can't be that hard."

But still she didn't say anything.

CHAPTER EIGHT

S hay hated that her vocal chords had frozen. Her brain, seemingly, too. Still, she felt like she was sifting through information so fast that she couldn't get a coherent thought to form into a word.

"I bailed you out last time," Austin said. "So this awkward silence isn't bothering me." He turned onto the road and pressed on the accelerator. Said nothing.

Shay's world narrowed to just this moment in this ritzy truck. A deep breath helped settle her thoughts. "I was a tomboy growing up," she said. "I'm sure that's not a surprise. I wasn't planning on going into the Army, but I've always loved working on motors and machines."

"So why did you go into the Army?"

A flash of regret bolted through Shay. How many questions would she have to endure during this date?

Relax, she told herself. This was what people did when they dated. They got to know each other. They talked. Shared important and intimate details of their lives.

"My mother had just passed away," she said quietly. "The ranch felt...too small without her on it. Or too big. Or something." All she knew was she couldn't stay there. She looked out the window, wishing she'd scooted all the way across the bench seat so she could steal from his strength while she spoke.

"So I enlisted and I left."

"Did you like serving in the Army?"

"You know what?" She looked at him and twirled a lock of her hair around her fingers. "I did."

He looked like he was going to ask another question. Instead, he closed his mouth and smiled. A cute, mischievous little smile that made her ache to run her hand along that bearded jaw and feel the joy radiating from him.

"So your turn," she said. "Tell me something about you that I don't know."

Austin's smile turned into a smirk. "I really hate mushrooms, and I'm terrified of snakes."

Shay half-snorted, half-laughed. "Snakes, huh? And you own a ranch in Hill Country?"

"I put on anti-snake cologne." He laughed, the sound of his made of pure happiness. She wanted to bottle the sound and listen to it whenever her anger started spiraling out of control. Not to mention the scent of his cologne....

"Right." She nodded. "It sure smells nice for simply warding off serpents."

A beat of silence passed before he said, "You think I smell nice?"

"Divine," she said before she could censor herself. A blip of embarrassment flew through her. "I mean—"

"No," he said, a twinkle in his expression. "You like how I smell." He leaned closer as if Shay couldn't already smell the musk and sandalwood and mint. Was that mint? "Just own it."

"All right." Shay chuckled too, relaxing further into the leather seat. "I'll own that."

"Just like I think you're beautiful."

Shay basked in the warmth blooming through her. The drive

into town passed in the blink of an eye, something Shay had never thought possible. While she'd loved living out at Triple Towers, the drive into town had never been her favorite.

But with Austin, she could drive for hours.

"So where is this place?" he asked when they reached the outskirts of town.

"It's right downtown. Turn right."

Austin complied and took them downtown. "I've never seen this place." He scanned both sides of the street and then looked at her helplessly. "Help me out."

"It's down the alley up there." She pointed up to the right. "Like a legit soup kitchen."

"Down the alley?" Austin eased to the side of the road, finding a parking spot easily enough because it was Monday night. "What kind of place is this?"

"It's a Soup Kitchen." Shay reached for the door handle. "C'mon, cowboy. Are you nervous?"

"To go down a dark alley? Yeah."

Shay laughed and got out of the truck. He met her at the front bumper, his eyes still warily watching the mouth of the alley. "Oh, come on, Austin. I'll keep you safe." She linked her arm through his and strolled down the sidewalk.

He moved easily with her, and Shay really liked this feeling flowing through her. She couldn't quite identify it, didn't know how to quantify it, but she didn't want it to end. He made her feel stronger than she normally did. More feminine than she'd ever felt.

She steered him down the alley, and he slowed. "There's literally no sign or anything."

"It's right down there. See that patch of light?" A rectangle of yellow light fell onto the concrete, and the door opened. A pair of women spilled out, giggling, and Austin relaxed beside her.

"See?" She tucked him closer to her as both females locked their eyes onto him. Then her. She pinned a smile on her face and kept walking. She didn't recognize either woman, but that wasn't saying much. After all, she'd left town for a decade and then sequestered herself on the ranch.

"Hey, Austin," one of them—a brunette—drawled, drawing a giggle from the other one.

"Oh, hey, Karla." He sounded sort of surprised and sort of like it really was nice to see her. A wave of jealousy and uncertainty clouded Shay's thoughts.

She pushed against it. Austin was a nice guy. So he'd said hello. It meant nothing.

He slowed and stopped and faced the two women. "I'm sorry," he said, sounding truly sorry. "But I don't know you." He had his eyes on the blonde woman at the same time he casually tightened his arm against his body, keeping Shay right beside him.

"This is Pearl," Karla, the brunette said. She had a pretty, heart-shaped face, and Shay wondered how Austin knew her.

"And this is Shayleigh Hatch," he said. "Do you know her?"

"Oh, sure," Pearl said, her voice as squeaky as a cartoon chipmunk's. "From out at Triple Towers."

Shay felt like someone had splashed ice water in her face. It dripped onto her chest, making her cold everywhere. She sucked in a breath as Austin said something she didn't catch. They talked, all of them, and she stood there, wondering how people would know who she was now that she didn't actually own the ranch anymore.

Come June, who would she be? Oh, sure. Shay from…. Who are you again?

Shay became aware of Austin gently tugging on her arm, and her feet stumbled to move with him. He opened the door to the Soup Kitchen, and a happy buzz of chatter and the scent of cream and mushrooms and chicken broth hit her hard enough to break her out of the stupor she'd fallen into.

"You okay?" Austin asked, gazing at her. With her heels, he only had two inches on her, and she nodded.

"Yeah. I'm okay." But was she? Shay wasn't sure.

Something flickered in Austin's eyes. Something that said he knew the exchange in the alley had upset her, but he wasn't sure why, and he wasn't sure if he should ask right now. He didn't, thankfully, and instead turned his attention toward the huge menu board that spanned the entire back wall of the store.

"Oh boy," he said. "I had no idea soup could be this intense."

She sighed, releasing some of the negativity and worry that had built in her system. She didn't want to concern herself with the future. Not tonight. No, tonight was about her and Austin, so Shay forced herself to look at the menu too.

"They have chili," she said, pointing to one of the left sections.

"Mm, I love chili." He lifted the arm she'd kept in her possession since meeting him at the front of the truck and slid it around her waist. The movement was slow, almost seeking her permission. A trail of fire erupted along the path he touched, and Shay found herself relaxing into his half-embrace.

"Are you really okay?" he asked, his voice a mere murmur with all the hubbub around them. "Because we can go somewhere else. Or back to the ranch. Whatever you want." His lips landed on her temple, and Shay wanted nothing more than to be wherever he was.

She had no idea how to deal with her feelings. She'd never let a man as far into her life as Austin had already gotten, and it was only their first date.

"I like the potato and sausage bisque," she said, her voice wobbly. How would he react when she told him things were over between them?

Relationships end in one of two ways, she told herself, the lessons she'd learned in her life flowing through her mind like hot lava. *Marriage, or a break-up.* And she knew that marriage wasn't an option for her.

So why was she even here with him, in her favorite restaurant, letting him hold her and kiss her? How had she allowed this to happen?

An inexplicable anger sprouted in her soul, expanding fast, faster, the longer she stood there, the longer Austin studied the menu, waiting for her to make a decision and tell him what to do.

In desperation, Shay did the only thing she could. The only option she could think of to slow this fury before she ruined everything.

She prayed.

Help me, Lord. She seized onto the prayer. *I like this man, and I don't want to hurt him. I need my job at the ranch, and if I'm cruel to him, he can dismiss me.*

She pressed her eyes closed. *Help me.*

"Mac and cheese chicken soup?" Austin asked, his voice incredulous. It also sounded very far away from Shay, though the remnant of his minty breath wafted across Shay's cheekbone.

She turned as if in slow motion to look at him. As soon as her eyes met his, everything snapped into place. She twisted against him so she could lift her hand and trace her fingers down his beard, as she'd fantasized about earlier.

He froze, but his eyes were so alive. Sparking and dancing and searching hers. She had so many things to say in that moment. *I really like you.*

I don't want to hurt you.

I'm not the marrying type.

I don't want to get hurt.

But I really, really like you.

She said, "You should try it. It's really good."

"You've had it?" He somehow made talking about soup feel like they were exchanging trade secrets.

"I think I've had them all," she said.

He leaned into her palm, which still rested against his cheek. "What's goin' on with you?"

She dropped her hand back to her side, but she couldn't look away from him. "I don't know." It was at least eighty percent true.

"Did I do something to upset you?"

Of course he had. He'd bought her ranch. Shown up all devilishly handsome, with those innocent blue eyes and that stunning cowboy hat. He'd worked hard every day since arriving at Triple

Towers, grown out a beard to cover his baby face, making himself twice as handsome and four times as attractive to Shay.

He had a magnetic personality that had seized onto her heart and refused to let go for six long months. He attended church every week, and now he'd infiltrated her anger management classes too. She had no defense against him, and all of it irritated her.

And yet, there she stood, close enough to his body to feel the heat, his hand firm against her back, indicating he'd like her closer if they weren't in a public place.

"I'm a mess," Shay mumbled. "I don't know what I'm doing here." She'd never spoken so honestly about anything before.

A couple of people moved around them, joining the line to order their meals. Shay felt eyes watching them, and she didn't care.

"Do you want to go?" he asked, his face falling.

Shay considered the option. Then she said, "No, we're here. Let's eat." She stepped out of his embrace, her body instantly cold. A shiver passed through her. Couldn't she enjoy one date with him?

He followed her to join the queue, kept his hands in his pockets now, and said, "So you'll never guess who's coming for Christmas."

"Who?" Shay kept her eyes on the menu board, though she knew what she wanted.

"My mother," he said. "And her boyfriend."

Shay spun to look at him, the dryness in his tone obvious. "You're kidding."

"I wish." A dark look crossed his face like a thundercloud obscuring the sun. It only stayed for a moment, and then the gloriousness of his light shone through his eyes again.

He nodded, that cowboy hat making him so beautiful it hurt Shay just to look at him. "Your turn to order, sweetheart."

She turned away from him, sweetheart reverberating in her mind. She generally loathed it when a man called her that, taking it as a derogatory term meant to make her feel inferior. But when

Austin said it, she felt like his sweetheart, like he said it because he treasured her, held her close to his heart.

As she put in her order, she knew she was in real danger with this man. The very real danger of falling in love with him. The danger of breaking her heart. The danger of breaking his.

CHAPTER NINE

Austin thought he'd worked from sunup to sundown before. But with he and Shay trying to get their regular work around the ranch done, as well as decorate all the buildings, the towers, the silos, the house, and the open spaces along all the roads, he felt like a zombie.

He woke tired. Worked tired. Ate tired. And went to bed tired, just to get up and do it all over again the next day.

But by the following Sunday—his day of rest—the ranch was ready to flip the power switch and light up the night.

At least he hoped so.

They'd tested all the lights, throwing away dozens of strings that weren't fixable. Fitting new bulbs into the ones that were. Dusting, planning, climbing, hanging. *So* much climbing and hanging.

"Everything's set for tonight," he said when he entered the kitchen to find Shane and Robin sitting side-by-side at the dining room table. She nudged her husband's coffee mug closer, and Shane patted her hand. They were so obviously in love, and Austin's heart pinched for a beat.

He wanted to share his life with a woman too. Sure, his

brothers were great, but they'd each found someone already. He didn't want to be the odd man out forever, and he found he'd already shared things with Shay he'd never told them. It was simply a different kind of relationship, and he wanted both in his life.

"Great," Robin said. "We'll be there."

"Tour starts here at the homestead," he said. "At least that's what Shay said."

"How are things going with her?" Shane asked, looking up from his phone.

Austin poured himself a cup of coffee, the memories of their Monday night date flowing through his mind. It had been almost a week, and while he wanted to take her out every night, it wasn't reasonable. Or feasible. They'd spent plenty of time together right here on the ranch. He'd eaten at her place on Wednesday night, and then skipped the anger management meeting on Thursday.

He sensed she needed some space. Or something. Things had gone great on the way into town. But something had flipped inside Shay as soon as they'd stepped into the Soup Kitchen. What it was, Austin didn't know. He was determined to find out, but only when Shay had softened toward him again.

"Austin?" Shane moved, the chair scraping against the tile to produce an annoying sound.

"Fine," he said. "Things are fine." He added sugar and cream to his coffee, keeping busy so he wouldn't have to look at his brother or sister-in-law.

"Oh, fine's bad," Robin said.

"No, it's not," Austin said.

"How did the date go?" Shane asked. "And you guys have been working non-stop all week. Can't be that bad." He looked at his wife and then Austin, who gave in and joined them at the table.

"She's...I'm getting mixed signals from her." Not that such a thing was new. Shay had been putting off I like you vibes for months, only to shut him down when he asked her personal questions, reject him when he asked her out, or stroke his beard in one moment and then separate herself from him in the next.

"The date really was fine. There was a moment that I lost her, and things changed after that." He remembered how she'd gone rigid in the alley, how he'd practically had to drag her toward the Soup Kitchen, how the talk after that had focused on nothing and everything. Nothing important. Everything little and unimportant —at least to him.

He looked at Robin, then Shane. "She said she was a mess, and she didn't know what she was doing there." His chest collapsed again, just with the memory of her words. Did she know how pointed they were? How sharply they sliced his heart?

"Maybe she's not ready to be dating." Robin reached across the table and patted his hand.

"What do you know about her dating history?" Shane asked.

"Nothing," Austin admitted. He sipped his coffee, his mind whirring. "And she's not real interested in answering my questions."

"You've asked?" His brother sounded concerned—classic Shane.

"Not that one specifically. I meant in general." Their week together since the date had been fine. "But she's not scolding me while we work anymore. She doesn't snap at me the way she used to. We're gettin' along great around here." He looked to Robin and Shane hopefully. "So that's good, right?"

They exchanged a glance. "Or it could mean she only wants to be friends," Robin said.

"Or that she just wants to keep her job," Shane added.

Neither of those options sounded good to Austin. They both punctured his lungs, making breathing difficult.

He stood half a second behind Robin. "I'll make breakfast," she announced at the same time Austin said, "I'm going to go see what's goin' on at my place." He gave her what he hoped was a reassuring smile and left his coffee mug on the table as he turned toward the front door.

"Let him go," he heard Shane say when Robin started to protest.

And go Austin did. Out the front door and down the road. Past the chickens and to the smaller house that sat in the crossroads.

Dylan had been working on it bit by bit, in between all the other projects on the ranch. Austin appreciated the new, bright white paint on the exterior. The porch on the front had been expanded and reinforced, and it was stained a beautiful, oaky yellow that made Austin smile as he climbed the steps.

There was plenty of room for a couple of dog houses, or a few chairs, where he could sit in the evenings and listen to the crickets or the clucking of his little chickens. The front door had been replaced and Dylan had painted the new one a bright blue that Austin ran his fingers down before entering the house.

It didn't look huge from the outside, but it was deeper than the eye could tell, and he thought there was plenty of space for a spacious living room. Right in the middle of the house, stairs led into a basement—that had never been used or finished, and which Dylan called, "a hazard of the worst kind," so a wall about five feet tall separated the living room area from the back of the house, where the kitchen and dining room sat.

To the left, stairs went up too, housing two bedrooms and a bathroom on the second level. Underneath them and down the hall past the stairs was a big master bedroom, with an attached bathroom, a small office, and another half-bath. The ceilings stretched to double-height in the living room and kitchen, which also added to the size of the house.

No matter what, it was way more space than Austin himself ever needed. He could live on the main level quite easily, and if he ever had a family, there were bedrooms for them too. He'd told Dylan to leave the basement for now, since the need to have it finished certainly wasn't pressing.

And they'd really only been working on pressing issues since they'd bought the ranch.

Things in the house looked great. New vinyl flooring stretched from the front to the back, a handsome dark wood color that made the light gray walls seem even brighter. With white trim,

Austin knew he was getting a modern interior for an ancient dwelling.

The kitchen didn't have appliances, but it was clear the electrician had been out to make sure everything was wired and ready. Carpeting supplies waited in the office and bedroom on the main level, and Austin found the same stuff upstairs. He tried the water in the bathroom up there, and it came gushing out clear as crystal.

"Getting closer," he said aloud to himself, to the house, to whoever was close enough to hear. Not that anyone was.

He couldn't hang around in this house that didn't have heat or air conditioning yet, so he left, bringing the door closed behind him, and went down the road a bit to the chicken coops.

The birds inside squeaked and clucked as he loaded up the six buckets it took to feed them each day. Then he let the first section of hens into the yard, where their throaty voices turned into squawks as he threw the grain to them.

Something about the way they walked—all broken angles and wild eyes—made him smile. Their necks didn't seem connected to their bodies as they pecked with such jerky movements, and he continued feeding them until all five sections had been let into the yard.

Then he took one of his empty buckets and went inside the hen house to collect the eggs. Some were warm, some already cold. Some were the color of cream, while some took on a darker hue of brown, and even blue.

He marveled at the eggs, each one of them magical to him for some reason. He hadn't been to town to sell them for a few days, and he decided on the spot that he'd go today after church. If he packed them under ice, they could sit in the back of the truck during the sermon, and he could hit the farmer's market in the afternoon.

"All right, ladies," he said to the hens when he came out from collecting the eggs. "Back to the coops." It always took several minutes to get them to comply, and he supposed he couldn't blame them. He wouldn't want to be cooped up inside when he could be roaming free.

He glanced down the road toward the cabins though he told himself not to. If he was going to go to the farmer's market after church, he'd need to let Shay know. He'd assumed they'd be riding to church together again today, which was probably a mistake.

"You shouldn't assume anything with that woman," he muttered to himself, turning away from Cabin Lane and lugging the bucket of eggs back to the homestead, where Shane's heavy duty refrigerator spit out ice cubes from the automatic maker like it had been storing them up for just the purpose Austin needed.

Before he went to shower, he sent a text to Shay. I have to go sell eggs at the farmer's market after church. Still want to ride together?

When he got out of the shower, he found the green light on his phone flashing. He'd gotten a text. From Shay: *Will we be back in time for the lighting ceremony?*

Of course, he tapped out. He dressed, refusing to dive for his phone when it went *ziiiiing!*, a special sound he'd assigned to Shay's messages.

Then I can tag along.

Austin grinned at the five words. *Great.*

Satisfied that the message he'd just received really meant, "I'm still interested in you, Austin," he finished getting ready for church and went to see what Robin had made for breakfast.

SHAY SEEMED PERFECTLY FLIRTY, FUN, AND FEMININE WHEN they went to church. She held his hand and cuddled in close to him on the bench. So close that Austin could barely pay attention to what the minister said. In the end, he still wasn't sure what he should've taken from the lecture.

She was capable, captivating, and cute as she helped him get the eggs displayed at the farmer's market. He didn't do fancy. He had a six-foot folding table he put a blue table cloth on, with a sign pinned to the front that said FRESH EGGS he'd lettered himself. He'd figured out he could buy egg trays in bulk and he had half-dozen cartons, dozens, and three dozen. He normally sold his eggs by the dozen, and usually in about an hour.

With Shay standing at the front of the table, wearing those four-inch heels that drank up the dust and a pulse-pounding sundress, the eggs were gone in twenty minutes.

Back in the truck, Austin wanted to clear the air between them. He felt like he'd seen two different sides to the woman sitting down the bench from him. One who was moody, sullen, and clearly dealing with the loss of her ranch—and probably a lot of other stuff Austin couldn't even fathom.

Surely she had friends she'd left behind in the Army. Her relationship with her father wasn't great, Austin knew that. And he suspected she'd never dealt with losing her mother either. So Shay was complicated, and she deserved to have a bad day if she needed to.

But there was also a sunny, sophisticated side of Shay that he'd seen several times. He really liked her, because she brought light into his life where it was the darkest.

"Thanks for coming with me," he said as she pushed her fingers through her hair. He watched her, completely captivated, only springing into action to start the truck when she turned to look at him.

"Sure." She smiled, such a simple action that made him ridiculously happy. "Anytime. That was fun."

"Have you been to the farmer's market before?"

A shadow crossed her face, but she cleaned it away quickly. "I sold a lot of my father's unopened items at the swap meet," she said. "When I was getting the ranch and house ready for sale."

"Oh." Foolishness raced through Austin. *Way to bring up something sensitive*, he chastised himself. At the same time, he hadn't known what she'd had to do. He only knew what she'd told him.

He navigated back to Grape Seed Falls and through town,

trying to summon the courage to ask the question he wanted to. *We're more than friends, right?*

But he couldn't say them.

What do you know about her dating history?

His brother's words wouldn't leave his mind either. He really needed to hear her say they were dating, and that she liked him, and that he had a shot at a future with her. Maybe it was too much for a casual Sunday afternoon conversation, but the craving to get the ball rolling in the conversational direction he needed it to go wouldn't leave him.

"I wanted to ask you something," he said when he made the turn from town onto the road leading out to the ranches.

"Sure."

"When my mom comes for Christmas with her boyfriend, I'd like you to come." He had no idea where the words had come from. They weren't even what he'd been thinking about. "And when I introduce you, I want to call you my girlfriend." He almost choked on the last word, especially when such a sound came from Shay's throat. Austin looked at her, heat rushing into his neck and face. "How does that sound to you?"

He wasn't comforted by the way her mouth gaped open, nor the way she blinked rapidly like she was trying to come up with something that wouldn't hurt his feelings. He'd seen that look before, after all.

"It's okay," he said, his voice falling almost to a whisper. "Forget I asked."

He hoped she'd jump in with, "Of course. That's great."

But she didn't, and the forty-minute drive back to Triple Towers was one of the most torturous drives Austin had ever made.

CHAPTER TEN

S hay stalked back to her cabin, her fire angry and burning and hot, hot, hot. Why did Austin think he could ask her about things—*girlfriend* things—without giving her some time to think? Time to process?

She'd had a great day with him. A fun ride into church, and wow, she'd enjoyed the hand-holding and the leaning into his chest while the pastor delivered a fine sermon on forgiving others. Shay wasn't super great at that, and she'd felt the need to get better. She would. Once she figured out how.

The chickens on the ranch laid beautiful eggs, and it had taken no time at all for them to get rid of all three hundred Austin had brought to the farmer's market. And then he'd had to go and ruin their perfectly good day with questions. With labels. With frustration.

She thought back to Thursday night's anger management meeting. Shawna had talked about self-training. Reasoning through a problem, finding your way through your specific brand of anger. Not only that, she'd mentioned training the people around you. She'd said she used to get even more furious when her husband would offer a solution to her problem.

"I didn't need his help," she'd said. "I just wanted his sympathy. His empathy. Not what I should've done or what I could do to fix whatever was going on. When I finally realized that—*and told him* —I stopped getting mad at him over something he really had nothing to do with."

Shay burst out of her cabin, the door banging against the wall in such a way that said she'd have to fix the plaster later. Didn't matter. All that mattered was finding Austin and talking to him. Lizzy and Molly trotted alongside her as she marched down the road toward the big house on the end.

She felt like her fists could knock down the homestead as she hammered on the door. "Comin'," a man called, but it wasn't Austin. Sure enough, Shane opened the door, looking sleepy and completely different without his cowboy hat. "Hey, Shay." He rubbed his eyes. "Austin's not here."

"Do you know where he is?" It was a miracle she didn't speak through clenched teeth. But this man was her boss, and she didn't need to give Shane Royal a reason to dismiss her.

"I figured he was with you." He looked over her shoulder to the ranch beyond. "He didn't come home after church."

"We've been back for twenty minutes."

"Maybe the hen house, but he did that this morning." He looked at her and shrugged, the hint of an apology in his eyes. "Sorry."

Shay nodded. "I can text him." She backed up a step before turning and practically flying down the steps. She didn't want to text Austin. She wanted to catch him by surprise the way he constantly seemed to do to her. "Come on, girls," she said to the dogs, and they happily came with her. Molly, the more sensitive of the two German shepherds drifted closer to Shay, finally settling her walk in step with Shay's.

She knew of two other places he liked almost as well as the chicken coops. His house and the equipment shed. He didn't normally work in either on Sundays, but only completed mandatory chores. But if he wasn't at the homestead, he had to be holed up somewhere.

Bypassing his house—it didn't even have appliances yet—she went for the equipment shed. The lighting ceremony was in only a few hours, and he was no doubt checking everything for the fifth time. It hadn't been hard to tell in the week they'd been working to put the Christmas decorations up that this old tradition held some meaning for him. Somehow.

Sure enough, she knew the man was in the equipment shed as soon as she entered. She wasn't sure how, but it could've been because she heard something rattle and bang near the electrical boxes on the south side. Or the lingering scent of his cologne in the air. Or the way her soul seemed forever called toward his.

He glanced up and saw her when she was still several paces away. Settling on his back foot, he gripped the jumble of lights they hadn't used in one fist as his expression darkened.

Face-to-face with him, some of her fury faded. *Fascinating*, she thought. Before he'd shown up at that anger management class a week and a half ago, spending time with him had been a form of torture. Seeing him and his brothers prancing around her ranch had inflicted her with anger so fierce she hadn't been able to calm it without help.

But now...she could look at him and come down from the fury inch by inch.

"What are you doin' here?" he asked. "Come to play more games with my head?" Bitterness and sarcasm dripped from every word, and Shay balked, unsure what to do with the emotion coming from him. He'd taken all of her abuse over the months, willfully submitting to her chastisement over the simplest of tasks.

Austin glared at her. "I'm not interested in this, Shay. I'm already mad."

"*You're* mad?" Her fingers clenched into fists.

"I don't want to talk to you right now." He pressed his lips together and lightning coursed through his eyes. "Leave me be."

She stalked a few steps closer. "Why are *you* mad?"

He gave her an exaggerated sigh, those eyes still storming with anger. "Because you keep giving me mixed signals. You're cuddling up to me at church, and flirting with me in the truck, or giggling as we walk into a restaurant. And the next thing I know, you've shut down, won't talk, won't even look at me." He flung the lights to the workbench and turned away.

Shay's heart shriveled, right there in her chest. She'd already hurt him.

"Why are *you* mad?" he asked.

"Who says I'm mad?"

"You came in here hissin' like a cat who just got tossed in a pond," he said, his head bent. "Not hard to see, Shay."

She let a moment of silence pass before saying, "I'm mad because I need more time to process things before I answer." She straightened her thoughts, trying to see past the anger. "You ask me questions non-stop, and sometimes I'm not expecting them. I don't know how to react. I need time to think. Or even a heads-up, like hey, I want to talk to you about being my girl-friend later. Okay? Then I have time to *think*. You give me no time to think."

At some point during her speech, he'd turned to face her. He blinked and said, "I don't ask you questions non-stop."

"You do," she insisted. "I'm...I'm not used to sharing my life with someone else. It's really hard for me."

The fire in his eyes cooled. "Surely you had friends in the Army. People you shared your life with."

"Surface stuff," she said. "You...you want me to go deep. You want me to tell you stuff I haven't told anyone, Austin." Her insides felt jiggly, and tears—actual tears—stung the back of her eyes. "Anyone," she said again.

They stood facing one another, glaring, for at least ten full seconds. Shay couldn't tell. It felt like an eternity. Finally, Austin swept into her personal space, taking her fully into his arms, just as her first tear leaked out of her eyes.

"I'm sorry," he whispered into her hair, his arms glorious and strong and perfect around her. "I didn't realize I was asking so much of you."

"I know that now," she said into his chest. "This is all new for me, and I'm terrified, and I—I—" She couldn't tell him she had no intentions of marrying. Ever. Not him. Not anyone.

He managed to keep her close and move far enough away to look into her eyes. He wiped her tears gently, lovingly, and she wanted to give her heart to him. But she'd seen what had happened to her father without his most vital part. And she couldn't give up that piece of herself. Wouldn't.

"I'm just a lowly cowboy from San Antonio," he whispered. "Playing ranch here until I figure out how to do it properly. Nothin' to be afraid of."

She shook her head, completely unable to explain. At least her blasted tears had quieted, but she couldn't quite look him in the eye and she let herself focus on his collar instead.

"Maybe you can tell me why you're so scared sometime," he said, gently pushing his fingers through her hair in such a way that lit her scalp on fire.

"Doesn't have to be today," he added quickly. A smile brushed his lips. "And I'd really like to have that girlfriend talk soon." He lifted her chin so she'd look at him. "Okay? You can tell me what you want to tell me, when you want to. But I should be clear—I want to know everything about you. Everything. Good. Bad. Ugly. Past. Present. Hopes for the future." He swallowed, a measure of fear entering his own expression. "See, I lied."

"You did?" Shay relaxed her grip on his biceps, glad she felt like she could support her own weight now.

He nodded slowly, seriously. "Yeah. When I said I wasn't interested in this. Big, fat lie."

Shay dug past the deep well of fear right in the middle of her gut. "That's what scares me the most."

He tilted his head, narrowed his eyes, clearly trying to understand. "You seem interested too."

"I am," she said.

"And that's what scares you."

No, not really, but Shay couldn't vocalize what lay at the root of her horror. At least not right now. So she just nodded.

"Can I ask you one more question?" he asked.

"Only if you're okay with me not answering it."

A flicker of light ran through his eyes. "All right. How many boyfriends have you had?"

"Two," she said, glad this question was relatively easy.

"And you didn't talk to them about personal stuff?"

"It wasn't like this." She tucked herself back into his chest, liking the steady *thu-thump* of his heartbeat comforting her in a way she'd never experienced before. "They were military boys. No one in the shop was interested in a female mechanic, and even if they were, I was too busy trying to prove myself to notice."

"So nothing serious?"

"Not even close to serious."

"Hm." Austin swayed slightly, and Shay moved with him, relieved and grateful her fury had gone from the raging animal stomping out of her cabin to this much more peaceful feeling of standing in Austin's arms. She knew which she preferred. She just didn't know if she could hold onto it for much longer.

DARKNESS FELL A FEW HOURS LATER, AND AUSTIN SAT BESIDE her on the front steps of the homestead as the first pair of headlights cut a path down the lane.

"They're here," he murmured. "I hope this works."

"We've tested it," she said. "It's going to work." But a trickle of trepidation tiptoed through her too. Four, five, six trucks arrived, and men started jumping down from the beds in the back and spilling out of the cabs. Shane, Dylan, and Robin came out of the homestead, bringing the scent of warm chocolate and sugar with them. Conversations started, laughter lifted into the air, and

Austin stood to help set up the table that would hold the dough-nuts and hot cocoa they'd promised.

Treats got eaten, and Shay got introduced to a bunch of cowboys whose names she'd probably forget before the lighting ceremony. But they all knew Austin, and he seemed glad they'd come. So she pinned a smile to her face and shook their hands, glad he didn't introduce her as his girlfriend.

"All right," Shane finally said. "Should we do this? We've all got to work in the morning."

"Work shmirk," Dylan said, grinning.

"We're ready," Austin said. He exchanged a glance with Shay, who nodded, and then Shane, who gestured for him to continue. "All right. Thanks for comin'. So the Triple Towers Ranch used to have a tradition of decorating the ranch buildings, fields, and homestead for the holidays. Townspeople used to come out and drive through as part of the festivities, and we've dusted off all the old decorations, added a few new ones, and we want to share them with you."

Silence followed his speech, and he smiled. "So give us two shakes, and we'll get this place lit up. You're welcome to drive around. The best view is out by the towers, but I might be biased."

Shay knew what he liked the best—the same thing she did. The huge star on the tall water tower. There was simply something magical about it, as if it truly marked where the Christ child lay in His manger.

Austin nodded toward the homestead and she followed him inside, through it, and into the backyard, where her two German shepherds were playing with Shane's sheltie and Dylan's shepherd.

"You ready?" Austin asked, locking eyes with her as he put his hand on the breaker that would send electricity to the equipment shed, which would send the power to everything they'd worked tirelessly to set up.

She put her hand over his. "Ready." Together, they pulled it down, and the loud clanking was followed by the buzz of electricity and then the roof of the house blazed to life with white, red, and green lights.

A shout went up from the front yard, and Austin grinned. "C'mon, beautiful. Let's go see it in the dark." He bent down and swept a kiss along her forehead before scurrying back through the sliding glass door.

Shay stayed in the backyard for a few moments, reliving that quick touch of his lips to her skin. Absently, her fingers drifted up to her hairline as if she'd feel a physical remnant of his kiss.

A wet nose met her hand, jolting her out of the stupor. "Go play, Lizzy," she told the dog before following Austin. After all, she wanted to ride with him in the back of his sister-in-law's huge truck, huddling in close to stay warm as they experienced the magic of Christmas on Triple Towers Ranch together.

CHAPTER ELEVEN

Austin had never seen anything so beautiful as his ranch all lit up. The sleigh on the roof made a boyish giddiness rise through him. The eight tiny reindeer weren't so tiny when he'd put them up, but they looked absolutely perfect poised in front of the sleigh.

Red, white, and green lights ran in stripes from the pinnacle of the roof to the rain gutters, the perfect accent to Santa and his sleigh.

"Let's load up," Austin said, and everyone started heading back to the trucks they'd come in. He looked around for Shay, finally finding her as she hurried down the front steps. He helped her into the back of Robin's truck, where Dylan and Hazel had already cozied up together, their backs resting against the windows of the cab.

Austin sat next to his brother, leaving a sliver of space for Shay, which she slid into, settling comfortably against his chest so they could view the ranch. Shane drove slowly, and the music filtered back from the cab through the open windows.

The snowmen pulsed in time to the song, something Shay had labored over for hours in her cabin after work. The chicken coops dripped with icicle lights. The cabins had all been decked out in a different color of lights that blinked and winked in time to the beat.

"Everything's perfect," he whispered in Shay's ear, glad when she seemed to melt further into him. He didn't see a single thing they needed to tweak or fix, and as the truck turned to drive past the towers, he held his breath.

He'd seen pictures of them lit up for Christmas, but witnessing them in real life, with nothing between him and their glory, was spectacular. One of the silos had red and white lights spiraled around it to mimic a candy cane.

Beside that, the star shone for all the world to see. Austin couldn't take his eyes from it. He wondered what it would have been like to be on the Earth on the night Christ was born. Would he have traveled to see the baby? Brought him a gift? He liked to think so.

A sense of peace so pure filled him. He closed his eyes for a few seconds, the imprints of all the lights flickering on the backs of his eyelids as he silently expressed his gratitude for the Lord, and for this reminder that he'd get to look at for the next few weeks until they celebrated the birth of the Savior.

"I love that star," Shay said, and Austin opened his eyes again to see they'd moved past the towers, the third of which was white from top to bottom—and had caused his back a lot of pain—with half a dozen lit up wreaths in various colors.

"Me too." He kneaded her closer. "Thanks for letting me be a part of this."

"Of course."

Back at the homestead, all the cowboys congratulated the brothers for the "awesome light show," and "great way to celebrate the season," before they took another doughnut for the road and headed back to Grape Seed Ranch.

Austin watched Dwayne and Felicity, his old bosses go, as well as Kurt and May who used to be his next-door neighbors. He missed them. Sure, Dean and Chadwell had come over from the ranch, and Shane had hired four new ranch hands. But Austin had spent most of his time with his brothers, and then Shay, and he realized he was still as lonely as ever.

Then Shay's delicate hand slid into his, and he seized onto it, using it to ground himself. And he didn't feel so alone anymore.

———

AUSTIN SLEPT LATE THE FOLLOWING MORNING, SURPRISED WHEN he woke and the sun was already streaming through his upstairs window. The house felt eerily quiet, and he swung his legs over the side of the bed, listening.

Shane would've gotten him up if he hadn't shown up for work, but Austin's phone said it was almost seven-thirty—about an hour later than he normally would've gone downstairs. His brother always had coffee on, but today, the kitchen sat cold and empty.

"Shane?" he called, glancing down the hallway that led to his and Robin's bedroom. "Robin?"

Nothing. A blip of anxiety pinged through him. He checked his phone again—no texts or missed calls. Starting toward the hall, his eyes caught on a piece of paper stuck to the fridge. It had his name on it, and he pulled it down.

Dwayne and Felicity called. Heading over to their ranch. Call you later. -Shane

Confusion furrowed Austin's brow. "Dwayne and Felicity?" What had happened? Were they hurt? He wasn't going to wait around for Shane to call him. He tapped a few times on his device and got the line ringing on his brother's phone.

"Hey," he said when Shane picked up. "What's goin' on with Dwayne and Felicity?"

"They got a call late last night, after the lighting ceremony. A birth mother chose them."

Austin stared out the window above the kitchen sink, shock and gratitude and relief mixing into a powerful cocktail inside him. He exhaled, a smile pulling against his mouth. "That's great."

"He called this morning and asked for help." Something clanged in the background on Shane's end of the line. "I guess they normally have a lot longer to get ready—a whole pregnancy. But this mom just decided overnight to put her baby up for adoption, and she's already in the hospital."

"Oh, wow."

"Dwayne and Felicity left to go be at the hospital with her in Austin, and we're settin' up the nursery."

"Do you need more help?"

"Nah. Dylan's barking orders like it's his kid." Shane spoke with fondness in his voice, the edge of a tease. Dylan loved kids and had often babysat Greta, Kurt and May's little girl, before the brothers had bought the ranch and moved. Austin knew he sometimes still went over there, especially now that they had a new baby.

"I need you to get the essential chores done on the ranch," Shane said, and pride swelled Austin's chest. Maybe his brother did trust him with important things.

"Of course, yeah. I'll get it done." Austin hung up and took a few more moments to enjoy the moment. Dwayne and Felicity were getting a baby—something they'd both wanted for a while and couldn't have alone.

Austin appreciated the miracles God performed for people, and he felt like the all-seeing being was aware of him in that tiny moment of time.

"Help Shay," he whispered, glad his first thought was of someone else and not himself. His mom would be so proud, as she'd spent years lecturing her boys to put others first. "Go to work and forget yourself," she'd said more times than Austin could count.

And so today, that morning, he followed her advice. He got to work, taking care of the horses, the chickens, the two goats they had—some work that Dylan usually did. He got Oaker and Carlos, Dean and Chadwell, Shay and the other ranch hands, all up to speed on what was going on, and then he sent them out to their jobs for the day.

He'd promised them lunch, so he called in a big order to Submarine Sam's, and went into town to pick it up. He made the familiar turn onto Grape Seed Ranch, going under that peach-carved sign and on down the road toward his old cabin.

May met him on the front porch and took one of the six-foot sandwiches. "Thank you, Austin. Busy day around here."

"I bet it is." He glanced next door, where he'd lived for four years. Everything was peaceful here, though a hint of excitement hung in the air. After everything was set for lunch on this ranch, May handed him a large plastic container.

"Shane said you've got yourself a girl." She smiled, and another ache moved through Austin. How he loved this ranch, with these people on it.

"Said she likes soup." She nodded to the container. "That's some of Kurt's famous chicken and wild rice soup. We hope she likes it."

"Thanks, May." Austin gave her a hug. "Tell Kurt thanks too." He went on back to his own ranch, repeating the process of setting up lunch for his own ranch hands.

Robin worked a lot, all over Hill Country. She didn't even come home some nights, but stayed out at different ranches and farms where she worked. Shane was great at making people feel like they mattered and they belonged, but he couldn't cook all that well. Better than Dylan or Austin, but nothing like what May or Felicity could do for the cowboys at Grape Seed.

Austin thought of Shay and her homemade spaghetti sauce, wondering if she might be the woman on the ranch that could bring everyone together with food.

But that day, he was the man with the sandwiches. Instead of clanging a big, metal triangle to call everyone to the table, he sent a group text, telling everyone the food was here. One by one and two by two, they came to the homestead. Just like at Thanks-giving, the house filled with chatter and laughter and chaos and love.

Austin adored the energy, and he caught Shay's eye before

ducking out the back door with his plate of food. She followed him, both of her dogs hot on her heels.

"How are things goin' over at Grape Seed?" She settled beside him on the bench on the patio.

"Seemed fine," he said. The air barely moved today, and the sky was cloudless and deep.

Shay took a bite of her sandwich, and Austin enjoyed the comfortable silence between them. He'd experienced lots of silence with her. Terse, angry silences. Huffy, annoyed silences. Out of all of them, he liked this quiet between them that didn't have any charge to it.

"I think I'm ready to have that talk you wanted to have."

Austin cut her a look out of the corner of his eye, not willing to fully commit quite yet. "Which one?"

"The girlfriend one."

That got his full attention and he put the last few inches of his sandwich back on his plate. "Yeah?"

Her smile broadcasted only a hint of hesitation. It was more of a smirk, a flirty grin, than anything else. "I don't reckon it would be a problem if you introduced me as your girlfriend—but." She enunciated the T sound harshly, another coy smile on the heels of it. "Only if I actually am."

He searched her eyes for an explanation and didn't find one. "I don't get it." He'd pretty much laid everything on the line between them. What else did she need?

"Well, I don't know what kind of women you've dated...." And she looked at him, those beautiful dark hazel eyes full of questions.

"Oh, you want the run-down right now?" he asked, surprised.

She tipped her head back and laughed. It was one of the most glorious sights and sounds Austin had ever seen and heard. He reached out and ran his fingers through the ponytail spilling down her back, rendering her mute and still.

Their eyes locked, and the now-familiar electricity between them pulsed and leapt, almost desperate to be let out.

"Not so fun to be put on the spot, is it?"

"I can tell you."

"Maybe later," she said, setting aside her own plate and cuddling into his side. He lifted his arm to put around her, creating another moment he wanted to memorize, never let go of. "I was just saying, I don't know what kind of women you've dated, but I don't really consider myself someone's girlfriend until certain… events have transpired."

"Oh?" Austin liked this game they were playing, but he hoped it wouldn't turn south on him in the blink of an eye, the way a few other things had. "What are these events?"

"You know, going out. Talking. Holding hands."

"We've done those things."

"Okay, let me clarify. Going out more than once. I mean, tons of people go on first dates and end things there."

"Are you askin' me on a date, sweetheart?" He pulled her closer, glad when she didn't resist.

"Yep," she said, no fear or shame in her voice.

"All right. I think we can do that."

"Tonight?"

Austin had no idea what the evening would bring, or when his brothers would be home. "We'll see if we can make tonight work." He desperately wanted to go out with her again, maybe get that kiss he hadn't gotten last time because she'd started out the date as his fun, flirty Shay and ended it a completely different woman.

"And, you know…girlfriends kiss their boyfriends." Her words landed in his ears and sank in deep, deep, deep.

"Oh," he said, his voice strangled and tight. "So you want to kiss me too, is that it?"

She straightened, removing herself from his embrace and leaving him cold and wanting. When she looked at him this time, there was no teasing sparkle, no depth of fear, no hint of sadness. She was perfectly serious when she said, "If you want me to be your girlfriend, I think kissing is required first."

Austin's mouth went dry, and his gaze dropped to her lips. He'd wanted to kiss her since the moment he met her, but he didn't want to do it in the backyard of the homestead, with eight cowboys just on the other side of the glass.

"That's comin'," he promised, his voice more husky than choked now.

Her eyebrows went up. "Yeah? When?"

"I don't know." He ran his fingertips down the side of her face, leaned in closer, thrilled and satisfied when she stilled and closed her eyes. "But it's comin' soon." It took every ounce of willpower he had not to kiss her right then, to straighten, to stand. "Come on. We've gotta get back to work."

She glared as she stood and collected her plate. "You're a tease."

He chuckled, swept one arm around her, and pressed his lips to her temple. "There. There's your kiss. Satisfied?"

"Not even close to it," she said.

He paused and turned his back to the house, positioning her right in front of him, protected from all the prying eyes inside. "I want it to be...better than this," he whispered. "Kissing you in the backyard wasn't what I had in mind." He curled the ends of her ponytail through his fingers, watched her until she softened under his gaze. "All right?"

"It had better be spectacular then," she said, a spark entering her expression.

"Oh, it will be, sweetheart. It will be." He turned and went into the house, hoping he could be a better kisser than the two military boys she'd dated. It had been a long time since he'd kissed a woman, and he'd never felt as strongly about any of them as he did about Shay.

He went to work in the fields, and it was a good thing the machines could practically steer themselves, because Austin lost himself and the whole afternoon to thoughts of kissing Shay later that night.

CHAPTER TWELVE

S hay felt like she'd taken all the pieces of herself, mixed them up, and thrown them into the wind. She had no idea where they'd land, or which ones would break which would get lost, or which she wanted back.

She didn't know much of anything anymore. Austin Royal had disrupted her life so fully that she was questioning everything she thought she knew.

Because maybe she was interested in falling in love.

Maybe she could give her heart to a man—the right man.

Maybe the outcome between them could be happy, not tragic.

Maybe she'd made a mistake by freaking out and shutting down over nothing.

Maybe, maybe.

May-be...may-be...

The word plagued her, pumped through her with her pulse, as she set the irrigation systems in the east sector of the ranch. It was long, hard work, but she didn't mind it. As a teenager, she'd worn headphones to pass the time, but now, she walked in silence along the footpaths between the fields, the peace and comfort that only came when she let the quiet into her soul finally arriving after she'd gotten the sprinklers in the third field started.

By the time she returned to the crossroads on the ranch, dusk was settling. Her back hurt, and she wondered if she even had enough energy to go out with Austin that night. A figure sat on her front steps, and she paused. Both dogs continued forward, undaunted and unafraid, but Shay couldn't quite tell who was waiting for her.

"Hey." Austin's voice reached her, and she moved forward again to join him.

She laced her fingers in his, beyond rational thought with the man. At some point after their argument and subsequent talk yesterday afternoon, she'd decided to be more reactionary with him. Less inside her head. More in the moment.

"I'm exhausted," she admitted.

"Me too." He squeezed her fingers. "And Shane is too, and he just got home, and he...I can't go out tonight. I'm sorry."

Relief rushed through Shay, and she laid her head against Austin's upper arm. "It's fine."

"Maybe I can get on home and see what's what, and then we can sneak away to look at the stars later."

"Just here on the ranch?"

"Dylan says you only have to take the ATV about five minutes away, and the sky is spectacular. Says it opens right up and the whole of the heavens spills out."

Shay nodded, her eyes drifting closed. "Sure. Text me." Sneaking away with him to stargaze sounded dangerous and romantic—spontaneous, something Shay never was. No, she was disciplined. Regimented. Routined. She didn't sneak away to kiss cowboys. Heck, she didn't usually leave her cabin after dark.

"All right." He exhaled, his exhaustion evident. "Let's get you inside. I'll be in touch." He kept her hand in his as he went up the front steps with her. He opened the door and let it drift into the house. Lizzy scampered inside, but Molly waited with Shay the way she usually did.

"There you are, beautiful." He smiled down on her, and Shay was sure he'd kiss her now.

Right now.

Now.... The moment lengthened, and still he didn't make a move. "I left something for you inside," he said.

"What is it?"

"A surprise." He released her hand, gave her one final smile, and went down the steps and on down the road toward the homestead. Left her kissless and alone, standing in the doorway of her dark cabin.

Molly sat beside her, panting. Forever panting, while Shay watched Austin until the darkness swallowed him. "What'd he leave, huh?" She entered the house, her nose working like her dogs, sniffing, sniffing. She couldn't smell anything.

She flipped on lights, closed the door, and immediately saw the plastic container sitting on the kitchen counter. She smiled and joy zipped through her when she saw it was soup.

From Kurt and May, Austin had written. She studied his handwriting, this note something already worming it's way into her heart. In a world with so many digital messages, having something so personal as a handwritten note made Shay feel warm.

It's chicken and wild rice soup. You like soups!

She giggled and touched the lid of the container as she continued reading. *I've had this one, and it's really good. I hope you like it. Hey, at least you don't have to make dinner now. -Austin*

She set the paper down, stuck the soup in the microwave to heat, and typed out a text to him. *Thank you for the soup. <3 <3 <3*

The heart emojis might have been too much, but Shay didn't allow herself to give them a second thought. She was grateful he'd provided dinner for her on this tiring day. And she did love him for it.

So she sent the text, fed her dogs, and enjoyed the chicken and wild rice soup before falling asleep on the couch, her phone tucked against her collarbone so she wouldn't miss a call from the man she hoped to call her boyfriend very, very soon.

A VIBRATION IN HER CHEST WOKE HER ONLY A MOMENT BEFORE the shrill sound of an old-fashioned telephone. Shay bolted upright, glancing around to find all the lights blazing in her cabin. A loud *thunk!* indicated that she'd dropped her phone. It continued to ring, and she scrambled to get to the call before it went to voicemail.

She swiped it on, her eyes catching on Austin's handsome profile picture, and said, "Hey," hoping she'd caught it in time.

"You were asleep," he said.

"I dozed off a little," she admitted. "I still want to go."

"Do you? You sure?"

Shay stood, already too-warm and partially drunk just from the sound of his voice. "I'm sure."

"All right. I'm at Dylan's now, and he's givin' me a lesson on the headlamps on the ATV. So I'll be a few minutes, and I'll come pick you up."

"I'll walk down."

"You sure?" he asked.

"It's a hundred yards. I'll see you in a minute." She hung up and scanned herself. The day's clothes would have to do because she didn't have time to shower or change. She did hunt down the thickest sweatshirt she owned and a pair of gloves. She'd driven an ATV plenty of times, and it could get downright chilly with the wind whipping in your face.

With that thought, she grabbed a hat too, a gray one she'd crocheted herself during a class at the church. She carried it in her hand as she left the cabin, telling Lizzy and Molly to stay. Beyond the circle of yellow lights cast by the porch lamps on Cabin Lane, the night seemed huge and all-encompassing.

Shay liked it. Liked the way it made her feel small and insignificant. Liked how it reminded her that there was something—someone—out there in charge of the universe. She caught movement outside Dylan's tiny house, with the headlights from the

ATV pointed east. Their low voices drifted on the silent night, but Shay couldn't make out any words.

"Hey," she called as she approached, hoping she wouldn't startle them.

They both turned toward her, and one—Austin—separated himself from the other and came over. "Hey, beautiful." He looked like he hadn't taken a nap, but he still seemed happy to see her.

When he turned back to the ATV, Dylan had disappeared. Shay saw the door close just a moment before the light was sealed inside the tiny house, and she laced her fingers through Austin's as they approached the vehicle.

"You've ridden one of these before, I assume," he said.

"Loads of times. My dad used to assign me to the herd. He said all ranch owners should understand their cattle, the fields they like best, their movement patterns, all of it." She gazed into the distance, remembering the long hours on the ATV, just her and the wild grasses. The cattle never seemed to do anything interesting, no matter how many months she tracked them, made notes, or talked with her dad. He put them on the same field rotation he'd been using for a decade, and nothing changed. Nothing at Triple Towers ever did.

Until her mother had died.

Shay shelved the thoughts. "It wasn't my favorite chore."

"What was?" he asked.

"Taking care of the cow-calves," she said. "I loved giving them bottles and listening to them bleat and then sending them out with the herd."

Austin grinned at her and swung his leg over the seat. She hesitated for a moment, admiring the width of his shoulders, before she sat behind him. Her arms seemed to know exactly what to do, though it had been years since she'd ridden with another person on an ATV.

But she held onto him tight and pressed her cheek between his shoulder blades. He started out slow and soon enough revved the engine until they seemed to be flying through nothing but black silk.

Shay started laughing, slowly releasing her grip on Austin's body. She flung her arms wide, keeping a grip on the vehicle with her thighs, her hair streaming behind her.

Austin slowed and parked and let her get off first. "You liked that, huh?" He cut the headlights and Shay's eyes struggled to adjust to the deep darkness that could only exist out in the country.

"Yeah," she said, almost breathlessly. "That was awesome." She finally found the shape of him just a few feet away, and she fumbled her hand in his. "No moon tonight."

He squeezed her fingers and lifted the seat where they'd just been riding. He pulled a blanket out and paced several feet away before spreading it on the ground. A great sigh came from him as he sat down, stretching his legs out in front of him.

Shay joined him, both of them easing to the ground as he put his arm around her and drew her into his side.

"Ah," he said. "This is beautiful."

There was peace in the stars. Beauty in the heavens. Comfort in his strong, warm embrace.

All of Shay's secrets threatened to flow from her lips, but she bit them back. She didn't want to ruin this wonderful moment he'd clearly worked to create. They were getting along great, and he didn't need to know about her issues. She didn't want to think about them. Obsess over whether or not she could give her heart to this man and not expect it back in mangled pieces.

She just wanted to be.

To be with him.

"Shay?" he whispered.

"Yeah?" She kept her voice equally quiet as if they were hiding from monsters.

"Wondering if now might be a good time for that kiss." His hand tightened on her elbow, and Shay twisted her face toward his.

Her eyes had adjusted enough to see the apprehension on his face, and a giggle slipped out of her mouth. She hadn't been this nervous since she'd left town and joined the Army without telling her father.

"I certainly hope so."

The witty, fun-loving Austin could've made a joke, but he simply reached up with his free hand and cupped her face, drawing her closer and closer. Closer still. She let her eyes drift closed, every cell and nerve and follicle tense, waiting.

"I haven't kissed anyone in a while," he admitted, his breath brushing her cheek he was so close. So close.

"Me either." She wanted him to just do it already. Couldn't he tell she was about to combust?

Finally his lips touched hers, a barely-there touch that made her shiver and shake. He formed his mouth to hers and kissed her like he meant it, and though all she could see was blackness, she felt like she was swimming in a sea of stars.

"I really like you," he murmured against her lips, kissing her again.

"I like you too." She kissed him back, her fingers slipping into his caramel-blond hair the way she'd dreamt of. She stroked his beard, and kissed him until she felt sure her lips would bruise. And she still couldn't get enough.

She had no idea she could feel this way about a man. She'd never experienced anything like it before, and when he finally broke their connection and tucked her back into his side, her heart was galloping like a herd of wild mustangs.

She closed her eyes again, reliving the gentle pressure of his mouth against hers.

"What are you thinking?" he asked.

"Nothing," she said. "I'm trying really hard to stay out of my head when I'm with you."

Austin shifted so he was facing her, cradling her in his arms. He pushed her hair off her face. "Still scared?"

"Yes."

He bumped his nose against hers. "Me too. But that was okay, right?"

She tried to search his eyes in the darkness, but they were just endless pools. "Austin," she whispered, trailing her fingers along his earlobe. "That was way better than okay."

"Mm." He growled and kissed her again, and Shay gladly went along with every caress, thinking this was the absolute perfect night, with the absolute perfect man.

CHAPTER THIRTEEN

Austin's headache ran deep, and the four painkillers he'd taken with breakfast hadn't touched the pounding behind his temples. If it wasn't for his scratchy throat, he'd just take more pills, drink more caffeine, and find some sugar and hope for the best.

But as he climbed up to the seat of the tractor, he knew he was getting sick. He hated getting sick more than anything else. He dashed off a quick text to his mother, who had a couple dozen home remedies for sore throats and headaches, and he waited for her response before rumbling out to the fields.

His phone vibrated, but it wasn't Austin's mother.

He hissed out a sigh, but his eyes had already caught on his father's message. What about Christmas Eve here in San Antonio?

Austin wanted to throw his phone as far as his muscles could get it, and he stabbed at his phone as he formed his response.

No thanks.

He had a whole lot more to say, including how exhausted this game made him, but he hoped he could get his meaning across with fewer words.

He sent the message, and this time his father called. Austin could've just ignored him, but he wanted to get things out and over and done. "Hey, Dad."

"I don't understand what's going on with you, Austin." No hello. No how are you? No nothing. Just a needling, half-whining voice on the other end of the line.

"No, I'm sure you don't." And he'd never cared before. His dad hadn't cared, because Austin had always done what his father wanted. He'd driven to San Antonio when Shane and Dylan wouldn't. He'd tried to get them to come. He responded to the family texts.

He'd been caught between two worlds for long enough, and he was tired enough trying to keep up with the life he was living. He couldn't keep one foot in a life with his father, because his dad only wanted him there when it was convenient for him.

"San Antonio is a short drive," he said. "You could come for an early dinner on Christmas Eve and be back to the ranch in plenty of time."

"You're probably right." Austin stared straight ahead, sifting through the angry things he could say to his father. In the past year, they'd surged to the surface, made him clench his teeth and hang up before he blurted them all out.

But now, he felt...annoyed, sure. But he didn't feel like he was about to go nuclear, and that was a huge improvement.

"I know you said Shane and Dylan won't come, and Joanna is fine with that. We just want *you* to come. You've always been so much fun, Austin."

Austin pressed his eyes closed, the seething fury roaring to life with just a few simple words. He felt like he was being ripped in half. His loyalty to his father and his family had always run through his blood. He'd trusted his father explicitly growing up. Had enjoyed working the ranch at his side, learning what he needed to know, telling jokes, laughing, and sweating under the sun.

He hadn't realized his father's betrayal when he was only sixteen. He'd been confused, everything happening so fast, that he'd actually been upset with his mother and his brothers for losing the ranch.

"I'm not coming," he said, his voice this freaky calm tone he barely recognized. It was the complete opposite of how his nerves rattled inside him.

"Austin—"

"Dad, please just stop. I'm tired of being manipulated."

"I'm not manipulating you."

"You are. You have for years. And I've let you. And I'm done." His phone beeped, and he seized onto it as an excuse. "I have to go. Mom's calling." He hung up, the urge to throw his phone still strong.

He managed to look at it and see that his mother had recommended tea and honey for his throat and more rest for his headache.

"More rest." Austin chuckled, wondering if his mother somehow had eyes here at the ranch that would know Austin hadn't been sleeping more than five or six hours a night in weeks. Of course she does, he thought. She had Dylan, Shane, and Robin. Probably some of the ranch hands too.

He thanked her and shoved his phone in his back pocket where he wouldn't feel it vibrated because the seat would be bouncing around too much. Then he got to work, wishing he'd brought headphones with him so he didn't only have his poisonous thoughts about his father to keep him company.

In an attempt to distract himself, he began to sing. He didn't have a wonderful voice, but there wasn't anyone out here to judge him, so he let the lyrics to his favorite country songs lift into the air. When he'd gone through all the songs he knew, he switched to hymns.

When he pulled back into the equipment shed and jumped down from the tractor, Shay walked toward him, a beautiful smile on her face. "Hey there, cowboy." She stopped and cocked her hip. "Heard you singin' out in the fields."

Embarrassment seeped into him, heating his chest and neck. "You heard that?"

"Pretty voice."

"Just what every man wants to hear." He gestured for her to come closer, and she practically skipped into his arms, giggling. He loved this happy, flirty version of Shay, and he swung her around.

"How was your night?" He gazed down at her, brushing back her hair and leaning down for a kiss before she could answer. He would never tire of her lips, and a twinge of electricity traveled down both his legs. Joy skipped through his system, and he pulled back before he got too carried away.

"Are we too tired to go out tonight?" he asked, half-hoping she'd say yes. His head still pounded and he didn't even know how to make tea.

"I'm not." She traced her fingertips down the side of his face, sending a shiver through his bones. "But you look a little worse for the wear." She wore concern in her eyes.

"I have a headache," he admitted. "And my mother said the best remedy for a sore throat is tea with a lot of honey. I don't suppose you know how to make tea?"

Shay bent back and laughed, both hands pressing against his chest as she straightened again. "Yeah, I can make tea. C'mon, let's go back to my cabin."

Austin held her hand as they walked down the spoke of the crossroads that led back to the epicenter of the ranch, then they continued toward Shay's house. Austin climbed her steps with her, and said, "My dad called."

"Oh, that doesn't sound good." Shay opened her front door and a rush of heat met Austin as he followed her inside.

"He wanted me to come to Christmas Eve dinner," he said, his mood darkening. "Claimed that he didn't care if Shane or Dylan came, that he just wanted to see me, that I'm the fun one."

Shay filled a teapot with water and set it on the stove. "What did you tell him?"

"I told him to stop manipulating me. Stop lying to me."

She pressed her mouth into a tight line and spun away from him. Several moments passed and then she said, "Good for you, Austin."

He approached her and slipped his arms around her waist, glad when she leaned back into his chest. "He makes me so...angry."

"I know he does," she murmured.

"I don't understand how a person can lie to someone they're supposed to love."

Shay tensed and stepped out of his arms, opening two cupboards before pulling down a large honey bear filled with golden liquid. The teapot began to whistle, and she worked in the kitchen, placing a delicate cup of tea with loads of honey in front of him a minute later. She got out a bottle of pills and slid it toward him too.

He sipped and swallowed, comfortable in this cabin of Shay's, with it's muted colors, and easy-going furniture, and those two dogs lying on the couch a few feet away.

"I want a juicy hamburger tonight," she said.

Austin glanced at her. "Is that right?"

"Yeah, that's right. So sip faster, let's turn on the lights, and then get into town."

"Where can we find the best burgers in Grape Seed Falls?" He sipped, the hot tea scalding the back of his throat. Somehow, he didn't think that was what his mom had in mind when she'd recommended it.

Austin thought she'd say Sotheby's, which was the ritziest restaurant in town. Or maybe Gray's, the hip, local joint that was packed at every meal.

But she said, "Burger Barn," with a totally straight face.

Austin nearly spat out his tea. "Burger Barn?" He shook his head. "I don't believe you." He chuckled and sipped some more. "First Soup Kitchen and now Burger Barn. I'm beginning to think you don't know what good food is."

"Hey, you said you liked the Soup Kitchen."

"I did. The chili was fantastic. I'm just saying the names aren't all that inspiring."

"Burger Barn has a California bacon burger that will blow your mind." She set her mostly full teacup in the sink. "Plus, they have sweet potato fries, and I'm *dying* for some of those." She batted her beautiful eyelashes at him, and Austin had zero defense against her.

"Fine." He gulped the last of his tea, the glob of honey at the bottom of the cup almost making him gag. But he forced it down so he could report truthfully to his mother that he'd followed her advice. "Let's go, then. Today's not a good day to die."

CHAPTER FOURTEEN

Shay kept the mood between her and Austin light, carefree, playful, fun, as they lit up the ranch and then left it in their rear-view mirror.

She did love the Burger Barn. The California bacon burger was to die for. And her mouth watered at the mere thought of sweet potato fries. But her stomach was not playing nice with the few sips of tea she'd swallowed at her cabin. How was she going to eat an entire basket of food?

Austin had every right to be angry with his father, if the stories he told about the man were even half true. His dad did manipulate him, tell him things that weren't true, all of it.

But wasn't Shay doing the same thing?

No. She physically shook her head as the word reverberated inside her head. He'd never asked her if she planned to get married. They weren't anywhere near talking about such a serious future together.

And she certainly wasn't manipulating him in the slightest. Her intentions for their relationship were simply...unknown. And that was okay. She didn't need to have a twelve-step program outlined with a man before they started dating. That was what dating was.

But his words had latched onto something sharp in her mind and they wouldn't let go. *I don't understand how a person can lie to someone they're supposed to love.*

She wasn't in love with Austin Royal, and he didn't love her. So they'd shared a couple of great weeks together. Several life-altering kisses. And before that, five months of general tolerance of one another, where her anger and mixed feelings had kept his advances at bay.

"So can we play that game where we tell something about ourselves the other doesn't know?" He glanced at her. "I'll go first, if you want."

Shay pulled herself out of her mind, satisfied that no, she hadn't lied to Austin, and no, she wasn't manipulating him.

"Sure." She smiled at him and looked back out the windshield, where the brightly colored Christmas lights people had put up on their homes, fences, and trees glowed in the distance.

"Okay, first the obvious one: I've never left the state of Texas." He glanced at her and in the dim light from the dashboard, she saw a hint of trepidation in his eyes, like she would care that he wasn't a world traveler.

"Have you?" he asked.

"Yeah, once or twice," she said.

"Where've you been?"

"Oh, let's see. Virginia. Kansas—there's a base there that does a lot of helicopter repair. I worked there for a few years. Hawaii, and Georgia." She'd ended her time in the Army at Fort Benning, and she did miss heading to the Gulf of Mexico for a few days of leave with her friends. She'd done a terrible job of keeping up with everyone she'd left behind, and she wondered if too much time had passed now to send emails and expect a warm reception.

"Hawaii." Austin's voice carried awe. "Wow."

"When I worked there, I had to become a member of the National Guard," she said. "It was only for a couple of months while they found someone more permanent." She laid her head back against the seat. "I did like it though. Pretty beaches, nice and warm."

"Which job did you like best?"

"The helicopter repair. I love things that fly." Shay had spent a large portion of her life wishing she could sprout wings and fly wherever she wanted.

"How long did you do that?"

"Just about five years," she said. "So almost half my time in the Army." She'd never realized that before, but now she realized how much she'd enjoyed her time in Olathe and Gardener. She let her head drift toward him. "Where would you go if you could go anywhere?"

"Anywhere?" He came to the T-junction and turned right to go into town. Several blocks passed and he made another turn before he said, "Probably Denver or somewhere with really tall mountains. The Tetons. Where are those? Wyoming? Not a lot of big mountains in Texas."

Shay nodded, appreciating his answer. "I think the Tetons are in Wyoming and Idaho," she said. "We should go." Where the last three words had come from, she didn't know. "I mean—"

"I know what you mean," Austin said quietly, yet the words screamed through Shay's ears. "So which way is this barn?" He looked left and right as Main Street loomed ahead.

"Oh, it's literally in a barn. On the old Harris property?" She looked at him with raised eyebrows, but he hadn't grown up in Grape Seed Falls and just continued to stare down the street.

"Head over toward Levi's boarding stable," Shay said. "Then you'll take Seventh and head out of town like you're going out to the state park. It's right on the edge of town in this great big barn."

Austin grumbled something that sounded like, "Great. A big barn," and got the truck moving again.

"It's a nice place," she assured him with a squeeze of his fingers. When they arrived, the dozens and dozens of vehicles in the parking lot backed up her claim. White and blue lights attached to every eave and edge of the barn set the Christmas mood, and when

Austin pulled open the door for Shay, the sound of Jingle Bells filled the air.

It was warmer inside than out, and Shay breathed in the scent of salt and pine, sugar and grease, suddenly hungrier than she'd thought. Pine wreaths hung on the walls, and the stage at one end of the space had big red bows tied to the front every few feet. Candles burned on the tables, and more white lights draped in elegant arcs in the rafters. The whole place felt magical and anything but like a barn.

"See?" She tucked herself into his side as there were easily four other couples waiting for a table. "This place is great."

"Yeah, I see." His eyes bounced from item to item, place to place, person to person before he stepped forward and greeted the hostess.

"Oh, hey, Austin." The woman smiled at him and flicked her gaze to Shay. "Two tonight?"

"Yes, please." Austin couldn't seem to find his voice, but he accepted the buzzer that would go off when there was a table ready, and they squeezed onto the end of a bench that was only big enough for one person.

"Do you want to look at a menu?" Shay looked at him, glad when he grinned and nodded. She got up to retrieve two paper menus from the hostess station, and when she returned, Austin had taken up all the space.

His eyes sparkled like stars on a deep black night, and he patted his knees. Shay settled herself in his lap and handed him a menu. She didn't want to make a big deal out of this seating arrangement, but it felt intimate and like they'd moved to a new level.

"California bacon burger," he read. "A quarter pound of Texas beef from local sources, Swiss cheese, bacon, tomato, lettuce, crispy onion rings, and avocado, with our special sauce." He lowered the paper. "What's the special sauce?"

"It's this mixture of ketchup, mayo, and pickles. It's divine. I could swim in it." Shay scanned the menu she already had memorized. "And the fried pickles come with this spicy aioli and it's also awesome."

"Oh, boy."

"What? You don't like pickles?"

"I love pickles." His hand landed on her waist, and a shot of lightning moved up her spine. She twisted and looked at the beautiful lines of Austin's face, finally settling her gaze on his. Another shock passed through her when she saw the teeming emotions in his eyes and felt them in her own soul.

The holiday music faded into silence. She could only smell his cologne, and it made her fantasies run wild. She'd been able to keep a tight hold on them for months, but now that she'd kissed him, it was all she seemed to think about.

She maybe moved half an inch. Maybe she didn't. Everything around her felt suspended in liquid, and Austin's lips parted.

The buzzer vibrated, breaking the moment between them. Austin startled, and Shay practically jumped off his lap. She slid her menu back into the shelf where she'd gotten it and followed the hostess without checking to see if Austin was following. Heat filled her face and she wasn't even sure why. Women kissed their boyfriends all the time.

But you're not most women, Shay told herself as she slid in one side of the booth and took the bigger, in-color menu from the hostess. Austin did the same, and Shay leaned her elbows on the table and leaned into them. "So I feel like you said you'd tell me something about yourself, and then I did all the talking."

She cocked her right eyebrow at him, enjoying the way his cheeks turned a darker shade of red. "You are quite the sneak, Mister Royal," she said.

"Mister Royal? Ouch." He chuckled, and she joined in, and together they laughed, a blend of sounds that had Shay wondering what else they could unite so seamlessly.

"DAD?" SHAY KNOCKED ON THE DOOR AGAIN AND PUSHED IT open this time. She hadn't been to visit her father much since Thanksgiving, but it had been less than a week. Still, she tried to get over to his new apartment several times a week to make sure he was eating more than canned soup and that his laundry got done.

Honestly, he'd survived for ten years on his own, but the state he'd fallen into was not one Shay wanted to see him return to. Since she'd been home, his cholesterol had dropped back to a normal range for a man in his late sixties, and his blood pressure had gone down twenty points.

"Vegetables!" she remembered yelling at him one day after they'd returned from the doctor. Her father had asked her what in the world he was supposed to eat if he couldn't have his beloved chicken noodle soup.

"Dad?" she called again, noting the stacks of magazines on the coffee table in the front room. How there were still this many print magazines still in circulation, she didn't know. Shay normally only allowed him to get a stack of four or five, citing that one person didn't need five magazines on-hand, not when the place came with cable.

He still didn't answer, and she noticed that he hadn't kept up with his cleaning either. Three pairs of slippers in varying shades of brown sat at the end of the couch, and alarm coursed through her. Was he ill? Why had she let almost two weeks go by without checking in with him?

A quick glance in the kitchen showed dirty dishes piled in the sink and beside it. So someone was here, eating. She turned away from the chores she'd complete before she left and headed down the short hall to the single bedroom at the end of it.

"Dad?" She paused on the threshold of the room, trying to see through the dim light to the bed. She'd come after her work on the ranch, after a quick spaghetti dinner with Austin at the homestead that could've used a lot of salt. But she'd eaten it and thanked

Robin. Then she'd kissed Austin on the cheek and made the drive into town to see her father.

A moan came from the bed, and Shay fumbled frantically to flip on the light. "Dad." He winced against the bright light but didn't really open his eyes. His head tossed from left to right as Shay rushed to his side. "What's wrong?"

She put the back of her hand to his forehead and found him on the feverish side of hot. "Have you had any medications, Dad?" She scanned the bedside table and only found ibuprofen. Thankfully. He'd hoarded prescription pills he hadn't finished, and thrown quite a fit when she'd insisted they throw them out.

"Sit up," she said, pulling him into an upright position. "Come on now. Wake up."

His eyes fluttered open, but they didn't focus. Heat streamed from his body. Shay pulled the blankets down, frowning at her father's flannel pajamas. Seriously, who wore flannel in Texas?

"Dad," she said sternly, trying to hold herself together and make a proper assessment. "I need you to talk to me. It's Shay. Wake up."

His eyes cleared, and he blinked.

She leaned closer so he wouldn't get distracted by anything. "I need to know what pills you've had."

"Just those." He gestured limply to the bottle of ibuprofen nearby.

"When?"

Pain twisted his features. "I don't know. What time is it?"

"Almost six-thirty."

"Six-thirty?" His eyes shot open. "I have fishing club tonight."

"Not tonight." Shay shook a few more fever reducers into her palm. "You're taking more of these and you need to eat something and then I'll decide if you need to go to the hospital."

"No hospitals. I'm fine."

"You're burning up and I could barely wake you." Shay started for the door. "Let me get you a drink, and I'll be right back." She hurried into the bathroom, which had been redone just before her father moved in due to a leak in the shower. So he had new water-proof tile that looked like wood on the floor, and a new toilet, tub, shower, and sink. She filled a glass with cold water and hunted around for a washcloth to make cool too.

She couldn't find one, and called, "Dad, where are your wash-cloths?" She knew he had some; she'd bought them herself. Almost everything in the homestead had been decades old, and Shay hadn't moved yellowed sheets, old towels, or mothball-scented comforters. All of that had gone straight in the dumpster she'd rented and she'd bought a few new linens and towels for her father's new, simple life in this senior citizen community.

He didn't answer—again—and Shay's annoyance shot through the top of her skull. She returned to the bedroom to find he'd fallen asleep again, and her frustration combined with her concern to make a deadly emotional cocktail inside her.

She woke him and made him drink enough to swallow the pills. After digging through the closet in the hall, she found the two washcloths she'd purchased for him—still with the tags on them—and soaked one with cold water.

She sat gingerly on the edge of the bed, feeling very much like this man's mother and not his daughter as she pressed the cold cloth to his forehead. He needed to eat, and if she could get his fever down, they might be able to avoid a costly trip to the emer-gency room. Surely he just had a cold or a slight flu bug.

"Dad?" she said, her voice tamer, her pulse calmer. "When did you get sick?"

"Yesterday," he mumbled. "Just a sore throat. Today...worse. Today's been worse."

"Why didn't you call me?"

He lifted one hand like he wanted to do something with it, but it simply fell uselessly back to the bed.

"I'm going to go make some of that chicken noodle soup you love." Shay didn't normally let the stuff into his apartment, but she knew he'd have a "secret stash" somewhere. She couldn't help the smile that touched her lips. Her mother had often spoken of her father's secret stash of candies, chips, and other treats while Shay was growing up.

Her mom had obviously found them charming, even when she found chocolate on the bed sheets or crumbs all over the counter-top. Yes, Shay's dad had an affinity for foods he wasn't technically supposed to eat, so he'd definitely have a can or two—or a whole case—of the canned soup Shay had banned.

Sure enough, she only had to push aside three cans in the pantry to hit pay dirt. As she waited for the soup to heat, the last of her anger faded. Not only the anger she had at her father for not calling her, but the self-anger that always took much, much longer to release.

But it was gone, before the soup was even hot. Shay marveled at that, wondered what was different about this frustrating experience that hadn't been before.

The microwave beeped, and she finished the food prep before walking down the hall to spoon-feed her father noodles and broth. Tomorrow was another anger management class. She'd be sure to talk to Shawna alone, see if she could figure out what she'd done differently this time that she hadn't been able to do in the past. After all, if she couldn't learn something from each experience in her life, why did she have them?

Another lesson from her mother, and Shay couldn't remember when she'd thought of her mom quite so much. And that didn't hurt quite as badly as it used to either....

As Shay once again marveled at this, she searched for an answer. The only thing she could come up with was...

...Austin.

CHAPTER FIFTEEN

Austin stepped into the equipment shed and heard Shay talking, her back to him. His first inclination was to step right back out and let her finish her phone call in private. After all, he'd seen the stiffness in those shoulders before, and nothing good could come of it.

He could also scent her anger on the air, and it wasn't a smell he liked on her. No, he much preferred the fruity florals she washed into her hair and sprayed onto her collarbone. Or the grease-scented shape of her hands as they stroked his beard.

But the words, "...of course I still want the ranch," made every muscle, tendon, and bone in his body seize.

Of course she still wanted the ranch. And he was a fool if he ever thought she'd want him instead of the land and house where she'd grown up.

His fury came instantly and hot, and it set his previously frozen body into motion. He stomped back out the way he'd come, making plenty of noise this time. He didn't care. He wasn't facing her, and he had no idea if she saw him or not. He slammed his hand into the metal door and exited back into the sunlight.

"I can't stay on this ranch," he said to nothing and no one. So he hurried away before Shay could catch him, could call him back and soothe him with pretty words and easy lies and pouty lips.

He didn't check with Shane about the truck. He'd already mentioned that he'd be going into town that night, so his brothers wouldn't be using the vehicle. Revving the engine, he tore down the dirt road toward the asphalt, desperate to put as much distance between him and Shay, who "still wanted the ranch," as possible.

He didn't make it as far as he'd hoped, but swung under the Grape Seed Ranch sign, almost skidding out he was going so fast. As he came to a stop in front of the homestead, he realized he probably should've called first. After all, Felicity and Dwayne had just come home with a new baby yesterday.

Surely they'd had a parade of visitors, and the last one they needed was a surly, angry cowboy who didn't work their ranch anymore.

And yet, Austin couldn't get himself to back up and pull away and leave.

He felt the exact same way about Shay.

Could she really be using him to somehow get her ranch back? And how would she even do that? He only owned one third of it, and his brothers would never sell. *He* didn't want to sell.

"What do you want?" he asked himself, staring at the front door. It opened, and Dwayne came out, squinting to see who sat behind the wheel. Recognition lit his face, and he waved for Austin to come in.

So Austin got out of the truck, his heart as heavy as his boot-steps as he climbed the steps.

"Hey." Dwayne clapped Austin on the shoulder. "What're you doin' out here lurking?"

"Just...." Austin didn't know how to finish the sentence, so he just shrugged. "Wanted to see the baby. Is this a good time?"

"Always a good time," he said, a smile touching his face, erasing some of the exhaustion Austin could plainly see in the lines around his former boss's eyes.

"What'd you name her?" Austin waited for Dwayne to open the door, and then he followed him inside.

"RayAnne," Dwayne said. "She's tiny." He took a few more steps and called, "Felicity? Austin's here."

A loud bang sounded from in the kitchen and a moment later, Felicity appeared, wiping her auburn hair off her forehead. She seemed flushed, harried, and Austin regretted showing up unannounced. But her face bloomed into a smile, and she came forward to hug him, which wasn't exactly their usual exchange. Maybe for Dylan, but Austin had always had a more formal relationship with Felicity.

"It's about time you came over," she said, drawing back, that smile still in place. It seemed genuine enough. "Come meet our little RayAnne." She led him into the kitchen, where the sweetest dark-haired, dark-skinned baby sat nestled in a bassinet.

Felicity gazed down at her and then carefully slipped her hands under the precious infant and lifted her out of the crib. The baby grunted and gurgled and her eyes opened to reveal the darkest shade of brown Austin could imagine.

He pulled in a breath at the wonder in this tiny human being. "Can I...?" He reached out his arms, as if he knew what he was doing. In reality, he prayed he wouldn't drop the girl.

Felicity passed the baby over, and Austin got a noseful of powder, which caused a smile to touch his lips. All of his anger quieted, and there was only this beautiful baby and his friends. His pulse returned to normal and he didn't realize how much tension he carried in his muscles until it released.

And while he didn't know what was going on with him and Shay, in this moment, Austin didn't need to know.

An hour later, properly fed an afternoon snack of leftover pizza and Ceasar salad, Austin stood from the couch in Dwayne and Felicity's living room. "You guys are great. Thanks for lunch. Thanks for letting me come crash here for a while."

Felicity cocked her head as if she sensed something he hadn't meant to say. With a jolt, he realized he had. "Why did you need to crash?" she asked, shooting a look at Dwayne, who now held baby RayAnne. He watched Austin with equal interest.

"No reason," Austin said, the lie loud.

"Things are going okay on the ranch?" Dwayne asked.

"Oh, yeah. Yeah, of course." Austin waved his hand like the ranch was the least of his concerns. In reality, he'd never worked so hard, and he couldn't wait to have his own place to call home. But neither Shane nor Robin had complained about him living with them, so he wasn't going to be the one who whined about their current living conditions.

"So it's Shay," Felicity said.

"No," Austin said quickly. "Shay is...Shay." As he said it, he knew it was true. She'd never pretended to be someone she wasn't. She'd resisted even talking about personal things for months. He had no idea who she'd been talking to, or what the context was. He wanted to find out, but that required questions, and Shay didn't particularly like those either.

"So what is it?" Dwayne asked.

Austin looked back and forth between the two of them. "It's me," he blurted. "I just get mad sometimes, and I need an escape."

"Like Shane," Dwayne said. "Have you tried his counseling app?"

Austin shook his head, the explanation getting stuck in his throat. He hadn't even told his brothers about the anger management classes, and it somehow felt disloyal to tell Felicity and Dwayne when Shane and Dylan didn't know.

"So what made you mad this time?" Felicity asked.

"Shay," Austin admitted. "She has a real knack for that." He gave them a wry smile. "I should be getting back." Especially since he'd be leaving again in only a few short hours and he still had an entire afternoon of work to accomplish.

He stood and gave Felicity a hug. "Thanks for the pizza. She's beautiful." He gazed at their baby one more time, grinned at Dwayne, and left them to themselves.

On the short drive back to his ranch, he practiced the

measured breathing Shay had told him about, but it didn't really lessen the pounding of his heart. Maybe Shay would've finished her work in the shed and already be out in the fields.

Of course she will be, he told himself. He'd been gone for almost two hours.

So he entered the equipment shed with sure strides, ready to get his fields plowed and ready for planting before Shane discovered he was a half-day behind. He'd taken several steps before he caught sight of Shay's streaked ponytail as she whipped toward him.

"There you are," she said in a snappy voice. "Where have you been?"

His defenses up, he slowed his step and stopped a good distance away. "I went to visit Dwayne and Felicity and their new baby."

"Why didn't you answer any of my texts? I even called." She didn't seem worried though. Just angry.

"I left my phone in the truck." And it was still there. He patted his pockets down just to make sure. "I think it's still there. Sorry." If he would've sounded more sorry, maybe her eyes wouldn't have flashed so brilliantly.

"You're sorry? We were supposed to go out to the herd to do the salt licks," she said. "I can't go myself."

Confusion made him frown. "No, the salt licks are tomorrow. We're finishing the field prep today."

She shook her head, her mouth in a tight line. "Look at the calendar." Her lips barely moved, and Austin walked away automatically, the way he used to when he'd first moved in and started working with Shay.

He paused, turned back, and said, "I'm not going to check the calendar." She wasn't his boss. Quite the opposite, in fact. "If you say it was salt licks today, I'm sure it was. I made a mistake." He took a step toward her. "But you shouldn't be so mad about it. It's a simple error." Another step. "What are you really mad about?"

"Nothing." She turned away from him, a classic Shay move that drove irritation through him.

"Right. Just like whoever you were talkin' to when I got here today thinks you still want this ranch. I'm sure that was nothing too." He scoffed, the sound almost a laugh though nothing he'd said felt funny to him.

She spun back to him. "You listened to that call?"

"I walked in and heard you say it. I was in the building for five seconds." He took another step, and another, and his height caused her to tilt her head back to look at him. "So is that what this was?" He gestured between the two of them, the fire racing through him boiling his blood into lava. "You thought you could make me fall in love with you, and then presto! You'd get your ranch back."

Fury colored her face. Or was that humiliation? Embarrassment? For a fraction of a second, he thought he saw her break, and then she covered it with her mask. The one she wore practically all the time. The one he'd gotten her to take off with him these past couple of weeks. The one he wanted to shatter and never see again.

But the mask was back, and firmer in place than ever.

He waited for her to deny it, but she didn't. He gave her time, remembering that she needed it. Shay was smart, deadly smart, but she liked to organize things before she said them. Which had been fine with Austin—until now.

Her fists squeezed and released, squeezed and released. So did her jaw.

Austin lowered his head, thinking maybe she'd be able to articulate better if he wasn't watching her so intently. His own negative feelings felt like he'd opened the floodgate and welcomed them in.

"Maybe at first," she finally said, her voice tight in her throat.

He whipped his eyes back to hers, sure he'd heard her wrong. "Maybe at first?" The words hurt him worse when he said them. "Wow, I—just I don't know what to do with that." He paced away, the need to flee as strong as it had been when he'd entered the shed the first time. But he wasn't his father. He wasn't going to run from the hard conversations, but meet them head-on.

Why was it so hard to breathe? He swept the hat off his head and raked his free hand through his hair and down his face. When his fingers reached his beard, he recoiled. He wanted to shave his face—right now. Go back to a different version of himself that couldn't get his heart shattered by three simple words—which weren't actually simple at all.

He turned back to her, drawing on his bravery to ask, "And now? What is this thing between us now?"

CHAPTER SIXTEEN

S hay pressed her tears back, choosing to be strong in this moment when she felt so weak. Austin was clearly doing the same thing, and she wanted him to understand. The only way that would happen was if she talked. He would listen.

"For a while there," she said. "I couldn't accept that I'd lost the ranch. Of course I wanted it back."

Austin simply waited, those eyes encouraging her to continue. "But of course that's not what I think is actually going to happen. And nowhere near the reason why I agreed to go out with you."

He folded his arms, his gaze steady, unwavering. His stance basically said, "And?"

"I was talking to an old friend of mine from the base in Georgia, and I haven't spoken to her in...a long time, and she didn't understand a lot of the family dynamics, or the mess I found when I got here, and I was just explaining, that yes, I wanted the ranch but well—" She shrugged. "We don't always get what we want."

She didn't want to lose Austin because of part of an overheard conversation. He seemed to be relaxing in steps, bit by bit. Keeping with her courage, she said, "I did not start dating you to get the ranch. My feelings for you have nothing to do with your *partial* ranch ownership."

He softened all the way, his arms dropping back to his sides and he released his breath. "All right then."

"All right then." Shay glanced around the equipment shed, thinking about the plethora of texts and the two calls she'd sent to Austin. He obviously hadn't read them or listened to them. If he had, he'd have burst into the shed, demanding to know if she was in love with him, not accusing her of dating him to somehow get the ranch back.

"Sorry about the salt lick," he said. "I honestly thought I was on plowing today."

Shay sighed and looked down at her hands. "Are we still going to the meeting together tonight?"

"Depends," he said.

She detected a flirtatious edge in his voice. "On what?"

"On whether or not you made that spaghetti sauce like you promised."

Shay tightened her ponytail, lengthening the moment before she said, "Well, then I guess we're goin' to the meeting together."

Austin smiled and closed the rest of the distance between them, sliding his hands around her waist slowly, deliciously drawing out the contact. "I hope we can always talk through our...problems."

Shay leaned into him, breathing in the fresh-air scent of his shirt, and pressed her cheek over his pulse. "I hope so too." In reality, she'd prefer no more hard talks like this. She didn't want to experience another afternoon like the one she'd just endured. Angry one second, scared to death the next. Another text. Maybe a call.

It had been emotionally exhausting, and the adrenaline coursing through her faded, leaving her sleepy and sluggish. She stepped out of Austin's arms and said, "I think I'm going to knock off early. Go take a shower and finish up dinner."

"Sounds good." He trailed his fingers along the underside of her arm as she backed up, effectively sending sparks through her bones and into her ribs. "I'll come by about five-thirty?"

"Sure, five-thirty's fine." As she walked back to her cabin, she knew that if she really wanted a future with Austin, she'd have to work at it. She'd seen her parents go through hard things. She hadn't understood everything, but she was an only child and had found out that her mother had gone through several miscarriages before giving up her dream to fill the ranch with kids.

She'd heard her parents have serious discussions when she was a teenager, and she'd heard them laugh. Seen them cry together, laugh together, worship together, work together. They'd been perfect partners for life—and then her mother's had ended so prematurely.

Shay wasn't sure she was up for the task of being in a relationship. They took a lot of work. She climbed the steps, Austin's face floating in her mind, and she decided right then and there that he was worth the work. Worth the time investment. Worth the tears, the laughter, the tired muscles, the sleepless nights, all of it.

"You'll tell him tonight," she told herself as she ushered Molly and Lizzy into the house. She shut the door and nodded to each dog as if making a pledge to them. "I'll tell him tonight. Tell him that I've never thought about marrying anyone. That I'm terrified he'll take my heart and shatter it." The more she spoke, the less sure she became.

She worried her bottom lip between her teeth and went to shower. With the help of prayer and hot water, she emerged ready to confess everything to Austin.

Please don't let me lose him over this, she thought as she dressed in a pair of black slacks and a blouse the color of bright pink bubble gum. Then she tended to the spaghetti sauce and set a new pot of salted water on the stove.

The simple actions calmed her further, so that when Austin knocked on her door, she was ready to face him. She answered the door in bare feet, with a smile on her face, to find him all cleaned up and smelling as delicious as her homemade spaghetti sauce.

Really, he shouldn't be allowed to walk around in public looking as good as he did. From the gray cowboy hat, to the leather jacket, to the dark wash jeans, he was the picture of male perfection. He ran one hand over his beard as if trying to hide his own smile. "Somethin' smells amazing," he said, pressing into her personal space, one hand easily slipping around her and holding her close to him. "Oh, here it is." He leaned down and drew in a deep breath of her. Somehow it was the most sensual thing he'd ever done, and Shay melted into him, taking her own noseful of his warm, masculine scent.

"Mm." His lips swept along her jaw before finding their mark and his kiss became real. He pulled away before she would've liked and said, "All right. We better spend more time eating than kissing if we don't want to miss the meeting."

Shay felt too warm and too soft, like a marshmallow over gentle heat, but she managed to turn toward the kitchen in time to see the lid on the pot start to jump. "Oh, water's boiling." She got the noodles in the water, set the timer, and pulled out a pitcher to make the strawberry punch.

Eating dinner at home had always been something Shay looked forward to, and with Austin joining her in her cabin, she wondered if she'd somehow stepped out of her stressed, angry life and into a new one.

With full plates of spaghetti and meatballs, she joined him at the bar. "So I had something I wanted to talk to you about." She twirled her noodles around, getting them all coated in the sauce made with her mother's recipe.

"Oh yeah?" He slurped up a bite of noodles. "That's new."

"New?"

"I usually ask all the questions," he said. "I'm usually the one who wants to talk."

A sting pinched in Shay's lungs, but she couldn't argue the point.

"I didn't mean it as an insult," Austin said, his voice at half-volume now.

"It's fine."

"Your whole face fell."

How he could keep eating during the conversation, Shay wasn't sure. The food looked good, but she couldn't bring herself to take a bite. "I'm fine."

At least a minute went by before he said, "So what did you want to talk about?"

Shay flinched, and she wasn't sure she could get the words out. Her mind seemed to be going in a dozen different directions.

"Hey." Austin put down his fork and twisted toward her. His fingers landed on her arm, drawing her focus there. She lifted her eyes to meet his, and she remembered all the feelings she'd had for him. She wanted to have him in her life. Today. Tomorrow. Possibly forever.

"I just wanted to...I don't know."

"Hey, it's just me," he said. "You can tell me."

Shay trusted him. *Just tell him*, she thought. But she felt like she was opening her chest and exposing her heart. Giving it to him— and he could do whatever he wanted with it. Crumple it up and throw it away. Shatter it and spread the pieces wherever he wanted.

She thought it would be easier to tell him she loved him than tell him she'd spent the last thirty years of her life as a woman who didn't want to get married.

But she didn't love him...yet.

And she'd actually thought she could say "I do" to him at some point in the future. Maybe a very far future, and he deserved to know that.

"Okay." She exhaled, any chance of eating before the meeting vanishing. "So my mom died when I was eighteen," she said. "It was life-changing to say the least. As I watched how my father reacted, I made a vow to myself that I would never get married."

Surprise burst onto Austin's face and stayed there. "Oh."

"I don't want to get hurt the way he did. He felt apart. Started buying things he couldn't afford. He became a hoarder, and you wouldn't believe half the things I told you about the homestead."

She could clearly see the ruined half-bath off the kitchen in her memories, which helped her push ahead.

"Because he loved her so much, he lost everything when she died. It may have taken twelve years, but he lost *everything* because he gave his heart to her, and when she died, so did he. I didn't want to end up like that. So I'd determined never to give my heart, myself, my life, to anyone."

With every word she spoke, she felt lighter, freer. But Austin's expression turned dark and then darker. He turned back to his food, but he didn't eat. "So we're just playin' house, is that it?"

Shay swallowed her fear, as well as her rising anger. She should be able to talk to him about things without him jumping to conclusions. "No," she said. "I think you're causing me to change, to think about breaking my vow...." She trailed off, her confessions all out now. She couldn't control the way Austin took what she'd said.

You can't control him, she told herself, another lesson she'd learned from her anger management courses. She could only control herself and her own actions, reactions, and decisions. Other people? Not her job to manage.

Austin spiraled another forkful of noodles into a bite and ate it. The silence between them felt like it could snap at any moment, explode all over her cabin and stain her life forever.

"So you're saying you like me enough to think about falling in love?" He kept his face turned away from her, his hat between them.

Shay appreciated that he could say things she couldn't. Convey them so concisely. She also liked that he gave her space to think by not demanding she look at him during the hardest parts of the conversation.

"Yeah," she said. "That's what I'm saying."

"I think I can live with that." He glanced at her. "I'm not doing anything casually here," he added. "I'm thinkin' long-term myself."

Shay felt like throwing up, but she managed to nod.

"You're scared of that." He wasn't asking.

"I'm still adjusting my thinking," she said. "So yes. I'm scared. And I'll need time."

"Okay."

"Okay?" she echoed. "That's it?"

"What did you think I'd do?"

"Break up with me," she said honestly.

"Because you made a vow twelve years ago that you'd never get married? People change, Shay. Isn't that why we go to these anger management classes? So we can change?"

Shay marveled at the wisdom in this man, and she needed the moment to be lighter than it currently was. She smiled at him, glad when he gave her his attention. "How'd a cowboy like you get to be so smart?"

"Hard knocks in life," he said with a straight face. "I've had plenty to learn, and have changed in a lot of ways." He indicated her plate with his fork. "You're not eating?"

"I'm not the one obsessed with this spaghetti sauce."

A smile spread across his face, and he tilted forward to kiss her. "I'll get you something on the way in. Should we go?"

"Sure." Shay left the plates on the counter and shrugged into her jacket. "Thanks for...thanks for letting me talk."

"Thanks for talking." He slung his arm around her as they walked out to his truck, and she slid all the way across the seat to sit right beside him on the drive into town, wondering if there was a more perfect man for her.

CHAPTER SEVENTEEN

The next day, Austin got the plowing done and went out to the herd with Shay, hoping to get caught up before he had to confess to Shane that he'd gotten a little bit behind. The hours working with cows and salt passed quickly, and he cleaned up and climbed back in the truck with Shay when his phone rang.

He glanced at it, expecting to see Shane's name and finding his father's. "It's my dad."

"Answer it," she said as she twisted the key in the ignition. "You can't change him."

Their meeting last night had been about transformation, and how the only person Austin could change was Austin. So while he wished, maybe have even prayed, for his father to stop manipulating him, Austin couldn't *make* that happen.

"Hey, Dad," he said. Shay swung the truck around and pointed it west, back toward the epicenter of the ranch.

"I'm not going to ask you about coming for Christmas," he said quickly, and Austin wondered if he maybe had started to change. "But what about this weekend?"

"This weekend, meaning tomorrow?" Austin looked at Shay, who shook her head.

"Yeah, tomorrow," his dad said. "We can go to the Luxury Lodge and just spend some time together."

Austin hadn't been born last week. He knew the Luxury Lodge was booked six months out, especially around the holidays. He felt perpetually stuck between what he wanted and pleasing his father, whom he felt some sort of sick loyalty to.

"We can go fishing," his dad continued casually, but not casually at all. He knew Austin loved the fishing off the streams surrounding the Luxury Lodge. "And hiking. Maybe hit a few golf balls."

Austin liked everything about the Luxury Lodge, from their big swimming pools to their acres and acres of hiking trails and fishing spots. It was the perfect place for a weekend of unwinding in the beauty of Hill Country, and Austin wanted to go. He just didn't want to play into his father's hand.

"Can you give me a couple of minutes?" Austin asked. "I need to talk to...Shane and see if I can get away for the weekend."

"Sure, call me back."

Austin hung up and blew out his breath. "My dad wants me to go spend the weekend with him at the Luxury Lodge."

"What's the Luxury Lodge?" Shay flicked a glance at him and back to the road. Him. The road.

"It's this great place out near Boerne. They have great fishing, lots of hiking and biking trails. A driving range where you can play all kinds of different games. Several pools." Austin shrugged like it was no big deal. "It was my favorite place to go growing up."

"So...maybe you should go. Is his wife going?"

"You know, I don't know. I assumed she was. He wanted me to come spend Christmas Eve with them, so I didn't ask."

"Would it be better or worse if she wasn't there?"

"I don't know. I hardly know her." And that was true. His father had gotten remarried only eight months after the bankruptcy and subsequent break-up of their family. At the time, Austin wasn't really sure what was going on, but he knew now that his father had known and dated Joanna before his divorce was final.

And when he'd found that out, the relationship between him and his father had cracked. It had taken another few years for it to break completely, and Austin wondered now if it was worth putting back together.

"So, what do you want to do?"

"I mean, it's *my dad*."

"Yeah."

"And you just don't give up on that, you know?" He searched Shay's face, wondering if she agreed or not. Shane had given up. Dylan too.

She'd told him a lot more about what her life had been like once she'd returned from her service in the Army, and her strained relationship with her father had come into more clarity.

Then they'd attended the meeting, and he'd taken her for a to-go container of her favorite soup from the Soup Kitchen, and they'd sat on the tailgate in her driveway talking until almost midnight.

He couldn't imagine the front room of the homestead filled with boxes and items that hadn't even been opened. She'd sold everything she could, and it wasn't even close to what they needed to keep the ranch.

Austin understood on a fundamental level. Though he'd only been sixteen at the time, losing the ranch that had been in his family for generations had been a blow he hadn't fully understood until the last few years.

"No," she murmured. "You don't just give up on that."

Austin looked out the passenger window, the landscape bumping by as they made their way back in. "How's your dad doing?"

"Better. It was just a cold. A little flu bug."

"I should ask Shane for the time off, shouldn't I?"

"It's up to you, Austin. You're the one putting yourself out there."

"He's not going to change."

"Probably not."

"I'll end up mad."

"Probably."

Austin exhaled, still torn and wishing he wasn't. His feelings didn't make sense, and that angered him too. "Can you drop me at the homestead?"

"'Course."

The rest of the drive happened quickly, with Austin inside his own head. As Shay drove past his house, she asked, "How close are you to moving into that place?"

"Dylan said I should be in next weekend," Austin said, a small balloon of hope lifting his spirits. "The appliances are in now, and he's just getting all the utilities turned on and then doing the final clean up."

"That's great. Are you excited?"

Excited not to be living with his brother and his new wife? "Yeah, I'm excited."

She pulled up to the homestead, and he turned to look at her. "Dinner tonight?"

"When will you go to San Antonio?" Shay seemed confident that Austin would go. "You won't go tonight?"

"I don't know." Austin was tired of saying that. "I'll call you later, okay?"

"Well, kiss me now in case I don't see you." She smiled at him, half bashful and half bold, and Austin adored the look on her beautiful face.

"All right." He slid across the seat and kissed her like this would be the last time.

An hour later, Shane had given Austin the same answer Shay had. *Do what you think is right, Austin.*

When he'd asked his brother if he'd go, Shane had said, "I'm not you, Austin."

"And no, he wouldn't go," Robin had said without even glancing up from her tablet.

"Why wouldn't you go?" Austin asked.

"I've never tried to influence you," Shane had said. "But I wouldn't go, because I'm not interested in having a relationship with Dad. If you are, you should go. There's no right or wrong answer here, Austin."

So Austin had called his dad back and discovered that he was already at the Luxury Lodge. No, Joanna wouldn't be there. Yes, Austin could come that night. He'd called Shay as he packed, and he called goodbye to Robin and Shane as he went out the front door. They could survive the weekend with just Robin's truck, as she was home-based until the New Year.

And that was how Austin found himself on the road leading back to San Antonio, actually looking forward to a weekend with his father. He found him sitting in the warm, rich lobby, holding his phone at eye-level instead of bending over to look at his phone.

"Dad." Austin stopped in front of him and watched his dad's face light up as he launched himself out of the chair.

He engulfed him, had always made Austin feel small though he stood just over six feet himself. "Austin." A booming laugh filled the lodge and he clapped Austin on the back several times as they hugged. "So glad you could make it."

His father's presence filled the entire space, drawing every eye. He always had. He was full of personality and charisma, and it was no wonder that he'd come back from the life he'd shattered.

Austin couldn't help smiling in his presence. It seemed nothing got his father down, nothing upset him, nothing rattled him. Austin envied him for that, and then remembered that jealousy was a quick way to anger, and he didn't want to go down that path.

"So," he said once his dad had stepped back and adjust his huge ten-gallon cowboy hat. "Where's Joanna this weekend?"

His dad's shoulders slumped, but he straightened them quickly. "Oh, she's off on a girls' weekend with her sisters."

A lie. Austin gaped at his father. He'd just *lied* to him. "Dad, what's goin' on with you two?"

"Nothing. She went to Dallas." He unplugged the cord he'd been using to charge his phone and sent Austin a mega-watt smile.

Austin refused to be swayed. "Is she coming back?"

The answer flashed through his father's brilliant blue eyes, and a flash of sorrow blitzed through Austin. "Dad. I'm so sorry."

"It's fine." His father waved like he'd taken a wrong turn in the city, not like his second wife had just left him. "It's fine. It's not the focus of our weekend. C'mon. Let's go up to the room and then we'll go to dinner." He started toward the elevator bank, and Austin grabbed his suitcase to follow.

He waited until they'd stepped inside the room to say, "What happened with Joanna?" He glanced around the room, which was clearly more than a basic place for sleeping. "Whoa. What's with the fancy suite?"

Burgundy carpet stretched in every direction, with a full living room before them, and doors leading off both sides of it.

"I upgraded when you said you'd come." His dad ushered Austin inside and closed the door behind him. "This room has a private hot tub."

Austin blinked and saw red behind his closed eyelids. Then green. This suite probably cost as much for the weekend as he and his brothers paid for a month on the ranch. And if his father had this kind of money.... The loss of his childhood ranch seemed like such a waste. He and Shane and Dylan had bounced around for nothing. Tried to find a place to belong because of their father's mistakes.

And you did, Austin told himself. First at Grape Seed Ranch, and now at Triple Towers. They were fine. Good, even. Maybe great.

His dad scurried around, pointing out the various amenities right in the room, and Austin wondered why he was trying to impress him. He stood there, in this luxurious suite he didn't need, and watched his father blow around him like a cyclone.

Austin felt his dad's anxiety, and he couldn't understand it. "Dad," he finally said. "*Dad.*"

His father finally stalled, came to a stop while showing off the espresso machine and looked at Austin with wide eyes.

"Slow down," Austin said, disconcerted that he was acting like the adult here. "Let's just go to dinner and worry about the gourmet coffees in the morning."

A smile flashed across his dad's face. "Dinner. Sure. I've got reservations at this great bistro across the courtyard."

A bistro didn't sound like the kind of food Austin wanted—and when had his father made a reservation? Confused, filled with adrenaline, and feeling very off his center, Austin followed his dad back down the hall and into the elevator.

By the time they sat down in the dimly let bistro, complete with a vase of roses on the table between them, Austin realized what was going on. "You had this weekend planned as a romantic getaway for you and Joanna."

His dad didn't look away from the menu. "I'd already spent the money. Now I get to spend the time with you." He grinned, but his eyes didn't settle on Austin.

He was still playing games. How Joanna had stayed with him for over a decade was a mystery to Austin, and he felt a little duped at the promise of a fun-filled weekend at the Luxury Lodge. His dad certainly knew Austin had loved this lodge as a kid.

Does it matter? Austin asked himself. They were here now, and they could have a great weekend without assumptions and manipulations.

"I don't want to go," Austin said. "But I don't want to be lied to either." He placed his arms over his menu, not having looked at it yet. He stared at his dad, willing him to look at him. Look at him now.

"I didn't lie to you."

"This was a romantic weekend with your wife," Austin said. "And when she left you, you called and asked me to come spend the weekend like it was simply father-son time. What would you call that?"

"Improvising."

"Dad."

"All right." His father let all the pretenses drop. "I just didn't want the weekend to be such a bust." He looked miserable, but Austin didn't want to feel bad for him. He made his own bed. He had to learn how to sleep in it.

"And I hate being alone," his father finished. "And no, Joanna isn't coming home. So." He blew out his breath. "I guess I'll have to figure out how to stand being with myself."

Austin had never heard his father speak so honestly, and it was a breath of fresh air. "It's a good thing to figure out."

"Yeah, I know."

Austin wanted to tell him about Shay, but he wouldn't be volunteering the information. His dad rarely asked anyone about their own lives, and Austin had learned to say, "Wow," and "Yeah," and "Oh," during their conversations.

"It's a good thing you're still single," his dad said. "Women are nothing but trouble."

Austin blinked, unsure of how to answer. He finally came up with, "Shane and Dylan seem pretty happy." And they did. So happy it made Austin see green sometimes. At least it had until the past few weeks, when he'd finally gotten Shay to stop fighting against her feelings and go out with him.

But he certainly wasn't going to tell his dad about her now.

"Illusions," his dad said.

Austin really didn't want to talk about this, and he decided to be direct about it. "Let's not get into all of Mom's faults right now," he said. "Or Joanna's." Because his dad would never admit his own flaws, Austin knew that. He picked up his menu. "What kind of sandwiches do they have here?"

By the time Austin pulled back into the ranch, he had enjoyed a couple of fun-filled days at the lodge he'd grown up loving. His father had made him angry a few times, but nothing Austin couldn't handle.

He couldn't wait until the next afternoon to see Shay, so he headed over to her house though it was dark and close to nine o'clock. They'd talked that morning; she knew he was coming home tonight. He'd texted a couple of hours ago; she hadn't answered.

So his steps slowed, hesitating to a stop when he realized there was an unfamiliar car sitting in front of Shay's cabin. A fancy sports car the same color as the night surrounding it.

She spilled out of the cabin, her laughter trilling into the sky, with a man right behind her.

Austin stopped, stone cold, his heart catapulting around inside his chest. He stood just outside the reach of her porch light, and neither of them saw him. She walked him to the car, all smiles and giggles, and he gave her a tight hug before climbing into the driver's seat and backing up.

Austin got out of the way quick when he realized the head-lights would illuminate him and show Shay that he'd snuck up on her again. He stood beside a tall tree trunk across the street and watched Shay wave to the car as it drove away.

In the resulting silence, her happy sigh carried to him. Then she turned and bounced back up the steps to her front door.

Austin stood in the shadows, wondering what in the world to do now.

CHAPTER EIGHTEEN

A knock sounded on Shay's door, and she laughed as she skipped back over to it. "What did you forget—oh. Austin." Her emotions spiraled from high to low and everything in between. "You're back."

"Yeah, I told you I'd be back tonight." He wore a stormy look on his face, and she wondered if something had happened since this morning, when he'd called. He'd sounded happy then, and had said things with his dad had gone better than he'd expected.

"I texted to see if I could come over, thinking it might be too late. But then I saw that guy leaving your cabin, and it's clearly not too late for male visitors." He didn't try to come in, though, but stood solidly in place, his hands tucked into his front pockets.

"I didn't see that text." Shay tried to control the shakiness in her voice. "Sorry, I had a friend over for dinner."

"A male friend."

"Are you jealous?"

"Of a handsome, unknown man laughing with my girlfriend?" His tone could've chilled water into ice. "Yeah, Shay, I guess I'm jealous of him. You've mentioned no friends."

"I have too. I was talking to one when you eavesdropped on me, remember?"

"I came in the shed and overheard. It wasn't like I hid out so I could listen to you talk to...whoever that was. You didn't even tell me her name."

"And yet you weren't jealous of her."

"*She* doesn't drive a fancy sports car or hug my girlfriend with a blissful smile on her face."

Shay liked that he kept calling her his girlfriend, but she really didn't appreciate his jealousy or his overprotectiveness or his possessiveness.

"His name is Robert Moss. He was my superior officer in Kansas."

"What's he doing here?"

"His grandmother lives in Austin, and he's down here visiting her, and he came for dinner." Shay cocked her hip. "Nothing happened. I don't *want* anything to happen. We're *friends*." She watched him as he held onto his anger, a stubborn streak in him she'd seen before. "So are you gonna come in and say hello, or just make me heat the whole ranch?"

He stepped inside, his eyes sweeping the space like there might be evidence of her infidelity. Shay smothered a sigh and offered him coffee instead. As they sipped, added more sugar and cream, and sipped some more, the silence between them wasn't nearly as comfortable as it usually was.

"I'm sorry," he finally said, breaking the tension in the room. "I tend to jump to conclusions."

"I hadn't noticed," she said dryly.

Austin gazed evenly at her. "I'm trying to apologize here. Could we cut the sarcasm?"

The sting in Shay's chest intensified, and she got to her feet with such a sudden movement, the stool scraped against the floor loudly. "I've got an early morning tomorrow," she said. Translation: *Time for you to go, Austin. And take your anger over nothing with you.*

He stood too, but he didn't move toward her in the soft way he usually did before he left. He didn't come close to her and lean down to kiss her. His eyes flashed with danger—anger—and he set his coffee cup in the sink before walking to the front door.

"See you tomorrow," he said before leaving.

Shay stared at the closed door, trying to figure out why things had gone off the rails because she'd had a friend over for dinner. She wouldn't have cared if Austin had joined them. In fact, she wished he'd been back in time to eat with them. She'd been dying to introduce him to someone as her boyfriend.

In the morning, she got up an hour early and got ready as usual. Before going to work on the ranch, she went into town to check on her father. He had recovered quickly from his flu bug, but it hadn't taken long for him to revert to some of his old ways when she didn't check in with him regularly.

"Dad," she said as she entered. The house smelled like scrambled eggs and syrup, his favorite breakfast, and she found him eating it at the dining table in the kitchen. "Hey, Dad." She gave him a smile as she picked up the stack of mail on the counter. Nothing here. Junk mail. Flyers.

She set it back down. "What're you gonna do this week?" She thought of her chat with Austin about fathers, and she'd made a promise to herself to try to connect better with her dad.

"Chess," he said. "There's a big tournament this week. And they've got some of the high school groups comin' to sing and play Christmas songs for us this week."

"That sounds great, Dad." Shay sat at the table with him. "What should we do for Christmas?"

For a moment, Shay saw the life in her father's eyes. The life that he used to have, before her mother died. He looked younger, like the strong cowboy who'd run their ranch, brought home penny candy from town, and taught her how to ride a horse when she was only four years old.

"I could set up a tree at my place," she said. "Or here. We could have a little dinner. Open gifts. Just something small. Me and you, and I'm seein' someone now. He'd probably like to come."

His eyebrows went up. "You're dating?"

Shay's face heated. "Yes, Daddy. It's normal."

"Not for you. You told me you didn't want to get married."

"I know what I said." Shay ran her fingers along her brow bone. "Look, it's Austin Royal, and he's a nice guy, so maybe he can come too?" She phrased it like a question, and she hoped Austin wouldn't be in a bad mood during their party. Because he didn't come across so nice when he'd heard something he didn't like, or saw something innocent he presumed was more than it was.

"Austin Royal? One of the boys who bought our ranch?"

"He's not a boy, Dad. He's thirty-three-years-old. And yes, he's the youngest Royal brother who bought our ranch."

His eyes lit up, and Shay could see the wheels turning in his head.

"It's not because of that," she said, shaking her head emphatically. "It's not, Daddy."

"But you could get the ranch back if you marry him," he said. "Just like I suggested."

Shay hated that the thought was still there in both of their minds. It was her dad's fault they'd lost the ranch in the first place. As she sold the things he hadn't even bothered to open, fixed up the house so they could sell it, and hauled load after load of trash out of the barns, sheds, and the houses, he'd been there, filling her head with strange ideas for how they could save the ranch.

In the end, they hadn't been able to save it. They'd had to sell it. And still her dad dreamed of getting it back. Shay had too, for a while. But that dream had died, and it remained six feet under though her relationship with Austin had progressed quickly these past few weeks.

"I'm not dating him because of the ranch. I *like* him."

"Some things can have dual purposes." Her father smiled and looked back down at his breakfast. "Oh, I'm out of eggs." Just like that, he was back to other things, like perpetuating a fake relationship just to get back a ranch was no big deal.

Shay left, telling herself over and over that she wasn't in a relationship with Austin to get the ranch back.

You're not.

You're not.

You're not.

SHAY GOT TO THE EQUIPMENT SHED EARLY, SKIPPING LUNCH TO do it, so she wouldn't run into Austin. She couldn't face him. Couldn't stand to think that, deep down, she'd never let go of the idea that if she and Austin ended up together, she would indeed have the ranch again.

She did her work in the fields, staying out a little longer than the job actually required, and put her tractor away as dusk fell. The light came on, the buzz of electricity filling the air and the soft glow from the nearby towers causing her to pause and enjoy their beauty.

She loved Christmas. Loved this ranch. She'd been working hard for the past six months, hoping that in six more, Shane, Dylan, and Austin would hire her on permanently.

But in order to really stay here permanently now, she'd have to be in love with Austin.

She wasn't even sure it was possible for someone to love her. She was prickly, and angry, and she'd vowed never to put her heart in such a precarious position.

But as she walked down the road with Christmas lights illuminating her path, she wondered if she already had.

Worry and fear filled her, making her chest as heavy as her footsteps. She caught lights on in Austin's place, with figures moving around inside. He'd said he'd be moving in soon, and the thought of having him just a few hundred feet from her front door was as exciting as it was nerve-racking.

She rounded the corner and found him sitting on her front

porch in the last of the day's light. Her stomach dropped to the ground and rebounded back to its rightful place.

His eyes felt heavy on hers as she stepped much more slowly than before. She joined him, tucking her hands between her knees.

"Didn't see you in the equipment shed today." His voice rumbled through the silence, oddly comforting in a way Shay had always enjoyed.

"Yeah, I was...." She searched for why she hadn't wanted to see him. Humiliation? Embarrassment? Anger?

"I went out early so I could have more time."

"Time for what?"

"Figure out what I'm doing."

"Did you figure it out?"

"Not even close." She turned toward him. "I think I just wanted to stay your girlfriend for another afternoon."

Austin said nothing. His hand slid across her knee and took hers. "So this is it, then?"

"Did you know?"

"I don't think *you* know," he said. "And maybe you should figure it out before we go any further."

"And we both need to be in a better place with our anger." She didn't want to tell him she didn't appreciate his jealousy. He knew. She didn't want it to be a deal-breaker between them either. She certainly wasn't perfect.

"I'm trying," he said, his voice broken somewhere deep inside him.

"I know you are." She leaned her head against his arm and squeezed his hand. "We both just need to figure out who we are alone, before we can be together."

"I know who I am," he said. "I know what I want." He shifted, glancing down at her. By the lights hanging on her eaves, she found the emotion teeming in his eyes. "I want you." His whisper filled the night, filled her whole world.

Shay didn't know how to be with him, not right now. "I need more time."

"I'll give you whatever you need."

"I need to know I'm with you for the right reasons."

Confusion filled his expression. "I thought we'd talked about that."

"I have moments of doubt."

He slowly slipped his hand out of hers. "You do need to figure that out. One thing I learned from my dad this weekend is that I'm not interested in a life that isn't filled with love, with dedication, with commitment to talking things through." He stood and took a few steps away, pausing to say over his shoulder, "If you only want me because I have the ranch, this ends here."

Shay couldn't assure him otherwise at the moment, so she let him walk away. Walk right down her sidewalk and out of her life. When she finally grew too cold to sit on the steps, she went inside, her heart a cold lump in her chest that neither Molly nor Lizzy could soothe.

CHAPTER NINETEEN

Austin perfected the dance that ensured he wouldn't run into Shay in the equipment shed. He either went really early, or he waited until he felt sure she would've been there and gone. He spent the evening hours he used to waste at Shay's—lounging on her couch, holding her hand, driving into town with her to eat dinner—working on his house. Dylan didn't need to run a mop around the place; Austin could do it himself.

After a particularly long day of work, from feeding chickens, to fixing the fences along the pasture's north side, to prepping his fields, he worked in his house to make sure he was ready for moving day.

And he ended up not waiting, but using some of those after-work hours to move his clothes and boots and hats over to his new place. He didn't have much furniture, besides the bed, but Shane said he could buy a couple of couches and a couple of barstools and a small table for the kitchen.

Austin spent Thursday night after work, when he would've normally attended his anger management meeting, wandering up and down the aisles of Fisher's Furniture, the best place to get everything in one stop. Dylan kept sinking onto couch after couch, exclaiming that "this one's nice, Austin. Come sit down."

Austin didn't want to sit down. He wanted to buy the few things he needed and get on home so he wouldn't have to be in town at the same time Shay was. He hadn't said anything to Shane or Dylan about the break-up on Monday night, so when Dylan said, "What happened with Shay?" Austin just shook his head.

"She told Shane she wanted to meet with him after the New Year." Dylan walked slowly, half a step in front of Austin, sliding him a look out of the corner of his eye. "What's that gonna be about?"

"I have no idea." Austin scanned the couch selection, a black leather set catching his eye. He crossed the floor toward it and sank onto it. Dylan sat on the other end and opened the recliner, his cowboy boots sticking off the end.

"Yeah." He smiled. "This one's real nice." He looked at Austin. "Right?"

Austin shook his head. "Right. This one's nice." He stood and flagged down the salesman who'd been tagging along behind them. As he started to look through the system to see what they had in stock and when it could be delivered, Austin tilted his head toward Dylan and said, "She broke up with me, because...well, for several reasons. Some are my flaws. Some are hers."

The salesman said, "I can get this out next Thursday between three and five."

"That's great," Austin said, barely listening as the salesman explained someone would call him on the way out and that they could check out at the big counter on the second floor if they had more to look for.

Since they did, Austin wandered over to the kitchen area in search of a table that would fit in the small space he had.

"So you'll fix things," Dylan said as if their conversation hadn't been interrupted at all. "And then get back together."

"I don't know." Austin ran his fingers over the top of an oak table. "We'll see."

"What flaws are yours?"

Austin didn't want to dwell on them, but he also knew he needed to do something to fix them. "Jealousy. Anger. Expecting her to talk on the spot."

"So don't be jealous. Stop bein' so mad. Give her time before she talks."

Austin rolled his eyes. "Y'all make it sound *so easy*. But if you'll remember right, I was the one who told Hazel we were moving and invited her to come. *You* forgot about her."

"I was stressed."

"So maybe I'm stressed right now." Austin didn't want to get into all the details. "I've been attending anger management classes these past few weeks."

Dylan stepped in front of him, forcing him to look his brother in the eye. "You have? When?"

"Thursday nights."

"I thought those were Bible Study classes." He looked beyond curious, his eyes searching Austin's for the truth.

"Well, I lied." Austin shrugged. "I didn't want Shane to get all parental the way he does, and I...I kinda just wanted it to be something I did until I figured out if it was beneficial or not."

Dylan nodded like he had some understanding of the situation. "And was it?"

"It seemed to be helping, yes." But Austin wasn't sure if that was true or not. Yes, his fury hadn't been nearly as hot as it had been previously. But how much of that had to do with the classes and how much with Shay? How much with Austin's own ability to be frank with his father?

"I still haven't heard everything about the Luxury Lodge weekend," Dylan said, deftly changing the subject as Austin signaled someone to get the table he wanted.

"Oh, I don't know if I can relive it," Austin said, his voice partly said and partly sarcastic. He shook his head and headed for the checkout counter. "He's...lonely. Joanna left him, and I think he's starting to realize what he threw away twelve years ago. That,

and that the way he feels and how people treat him is *his* fault."
Austin gave Dylan a half a smile, all he could muster at the
moment. "Or maybe that's just wishful thinking on my part."

He paid for the furniture and he asked Dylan if he wanted to
go to Burger Barn.

"Seriously?" Dylan asked.

"Seriously. They have fried pickles that are amazing, and the
sweet potato fries...." He smacked his lips. "You'll love them."

AUSTIN DIDN'T MEAN TO STAND ON HIS BACK DECK AND FACE
Shay's house as the sun rose on the Sabbath. Somehow, his feet had
simply brought him here. The air held a holiday crispness that
Austin's coffee mug kept off his fingers. He sipped, watching her
house for signs of life.

The cabins had back doors, and when he saw her two German
shepherds run between the cabins, he knew she'd let them out
back there. If she came around the corner, he'd duck back inside.
Because surely she could see his back deck if she chose to look.

She probably wouldn't choose to look though. She hadn't been
happy with his jealousy, and Austin hadn't either. But Shay had
literally mentioned no friends. Heck, she'd hardly spoken of her
time in the Army at all, only saying something when he pried it out
of her.

And did he really want to be with someone who thought a
conversation was explaining how to fix a baler?

He shook his head, his heart hanging heavily in his chest, and
went back inside before Shay caught him pining for her on his
back deck.

He'd spoken true when he'd told her he wanted her. He'd said,
"I want you," but he could've just as easily said, "I love you."

He wasn't entirely sure, because Austin had never been in love
before. But his pulse quickened when he thought of Shay, even

now. He couldn't imagine living on this ranch with her, but without her to hold hands with, talk to, kiss goodnight.

He liked that she wasn't perfect. That her life hadn't been constructed with sunshine and unicorns. That she'd made something of herself, picked up pieces when they broke, and kept trying. She inspired him to do the same thing, and he settled at the bar, because the other furniture wouldn't be delivered until later in the week.

With his laptop open, he navigated to the online anger management group he'd found. They had articles, videos, and a forum where people could talk. Austin could read something he'd been thinking about. Watch a video to help him learn coping strategies. Post in the forum and interact with others.

The online group wasn't where he really wanted to be, but he couldn't insert himself into Shay's meetings. Not again. Not until he knew for sure that she wanted him for him and not because he came with one-third of the ranch.

He'd learned so much already, and he wasn't angry with Shay. Or himself. Or his father. Austin felt a keen sense of acceptance for who they all were—children of God—and a thick blanket of peace fell over him.

He closed the laptop without reading or watching or posting, and moved over to a box he'd hidden away. He'd found it in the shed when he and Shay had gone through the Christmas decorations and put it in the house weeks ago.

It held photographs of earlier times on the ranch. There had been an entire album of the Christmas lights all lit up on the top, which was probably how the box had ended up in the shed. He moved that book aside, having already looked at all those beautiful pictures. Triple Towers had been featured in the Texas Hill Country magazine at one point, and the same fondness he'd felt when he'd see the article filtered through him now.

The photos underneath were loose, and in no particular order. There were a lot of smiling faces he didn't recognize—ranch hands throughout the years. His eye caught on one that looked like a family, and he curled his fingers around it.

His breath caught in his throat, and he knew exactly what to do with this picture. Pinching it tightly, he walked back onto the deck and gazed at Shay's house. Would she like to see it again? Would it remind her of happier times on the ranch?

The little girl in the picture—clearly Shay—was smiling so widely it looked like her face might crack. Her mother and father crouched behind her, both of them wearing radiant grins too. This was clearly a celebration to remember, something grand, because the joy exuded from the picture and filled Austin's whole soul.

Her front door opened, and Austin scampered back into the house, nearly dropping the photograph in the process. He set it carefully back in the box and went to get ready for church. He never thought he'd enjoy making the drive on Sunday mornings with Shay, but he had. So much. So much it made his chest ache when he had to do it alone.

Church was boring, mostly because he couldn't focus so the sermon seemed to go on and on. He couldn't bear to go back to his house, though he'd been looking forward to living in it for months now. Alone. He thought that was what he wanted.

How wrong he'd been.

Now that he had a taste of life with Shay, he wanted her in the house with him, the scent of homemade spaghetti sauce filling the air as they talked about the ranch, the upcoming holidays, their fathers.

He drove past the turn-off to the ranch, wondering how far west he could get on this road. He let his mind wander, finding some relief from the barrage of thoughts that had been plaguing him since she'd broken up with him almost a week ago.

With only another week until Christmas, Austin wondered if he should call his dad and go to San Antonio. At the very least, he and his brothers should invite their dad up to the festivities at the ranch, especially with Joanna gone now.

Please help me know what to do, Austin prayed. He felt like he'd tossed several balls into the air—the ranch, Shay, his anger, his jealousy, his father—and they were all headed down. He had no idea if he could catch them all or not, and he felt like something important was going to shatter.

Get on home and talk to Shane and Dylan.

He wasn't sure if the thought came from him or God, but he swung the truck around and headed back to the ranch. He didn't knock as he went into the homestead, and the sound of his brothers' laughter met his ears.

A smile popped onto his face too, and he joined them in the kitchen, where Robin stood at the counter with two pizzas in front of her, laughing too. Hazel came down the hall, her eyes as curious as Austin felt.

"What's got y'all laughing so hard?" he asked.

There was something familial about the scene, and how perfectly Austin fit into it, like the last puzzle piece that had been missing for a while. He glanced around, more at home now than he'd been anywhere else, and this ranch held a hint of the divine in the very air. He loved it.

"Oh, nothing," Shane said, standing up to cut the pizzas. "Where you been?"

"Church."

"We went too," Shane said. "And we've been home for forty minutes."

"Drivin' around."

"Figuring out how to get Shay back," Dylan added as he stepped over to Hazel and swept his arm around her. Their love was almost cute, and Austin almost didn't feel a pang of longing so strongly that his muscles tensed.

"Some of that," Austin admitted. "And I was also thinkin' maybe we should invite Dad to the ranch for Christmas...." He let his words hang there, hoping his brothers would experience a softening of the heart.

The last of Shane's smile faded, and Dylan fell quiet. He'd look to Shane for his lead, and Austin usually did too. But in this, he wanted his voice to be heard.

"Joanna left him, and I just think it would be...prudent for us to extend the olive branch this holiday season. He shouldn't be alone."

"He shouldn't have done a lot of things." Shane sliced through the first pizza with quick strokes while Robin busied herself with opening a bag of salad.

"I'm not saying he's perfect, or that anything he's done is right," Austin said. "I'm saying, maybe he deserves another chance." He looked at everyone standing in the room. "Don't you think people deserve more than one chance?"

Hazel nudged Dylan and said, "I gave you more than one chance."

"We've all had more than one chance," Robin said. "Shane asked me out several times before I said yes." She bumped into him with her hip. "Best thing I ever did. I'm glad he didn't give up on me."

"Oh, come on," Shane said, his eyes flashing with lightning. "Those second chances are completely different than what our dad did. The man cheated on his wife and bankrupted our ranch. Then he left us to fend for ourselves, take care of our mother, and figure out our own way in the world."

Silence followed Shane's words, and Austin felt the truth of them way down in his soul. They used to make him so angry he couldn't see straight. But now.... Now he just felt sorry for his father.

"And look where we ended up," he said through a tight throat. "Together. Two of us happy and in love. This great ranch we're working together, where we won't repeat those mistakes, where our kids can grow up, and hopefully inherit this place when our time on Earth is up."

Shane shook his head. "All three of us could be happy in love if he'd stop bein' so stubborn."

Austin felt like he'd been hit with ice water in the face. "That's not true. It's not me who's holding things back with Shay."

"No?" Shane put the pizza cutter in the sink and faced Austin. "I believe Dylan said some of the issues were yours."

"They are, of course," he said. "But Shay's the one who has to decide if she wants to be with me because it's me, or because I can give her the ranch she lost."

His words landed harshly in the kitchen, making every eye turn round.

"She's not a bad person," he said quickly. "But I told her if what we had was just about the ranch, it's over." And he miserable from head to toe at the very thought. He cleared his throat, his stomach suddenly providing the perfect escape from this conversation by growling loudly.

"Can we eat? I'm starving." He practically lunged for a paper plate and loaded it with five slices of pizza, skipping the salad completely. "And can we at least all think about inviting Dad for Christmas? Maybe we can talk about it again in a couple of days."

"Let's say grace," Shane said, taking Austin's plate. "Then we can eat."

"And we'll think about inviting Dad." Dylan stepped next to Shane. "Right, Shane. We'll think about it?"

And while Shane certainly didn't look like he'd think about it, he said, "Sure, I'll think about it."

Austin enjoyed the rest of the afternoon with his family, but he didn't stay as long as he would have if he'd still lived in the homestead. He couldn't help feeling like the fifth wheel, and how everything would be better if Shay were beside him.

And he knew: *She* was the missing piece in his life. The final piece that would make the jumbled mess of his life complete.

CHAPTER TWENTY

Shay only had seven more days until Christmas. She'd been unable to get her father to commit to a Hatch Family Christmas, and she'd finally discovered the reason why: He'd been invited out to the ranch for their celebrations.

Of course he had. The Royal Brothers were kind to him, invited him to their family functions, and actually acted like they liked having him around. They probably did.

Shay had also been invited to the Christmas Eve gift opening, as well as the big meal on Christmas Day. Shane had talked to her the week before. Surely he knew she'd broken up with Austin, but if he did, Shane made no indication of it. She wished it had been Austin informing her of the dates and times and activities of the holidays on the ranch. Austin, not Shane.

She wanted to attend everything, badly, especially once she learned that her father wasn't particularly interested in setting up a tree in his apartment and having a meal just with her. Now that Austin was waiting on the backburner, she couldn't very well invite him.

She left the ranch at lunchtime on Monday, intending to spend the time she normally did with Austin in the equipment shed shopping on Main Street instead. She didn't have a single gift for anyone, and though her list wasn't extensive, it would still take most of the afternoon to get everything she needed.

She always bought chocolate for the ranch hands, a tradition her great-grandfather had started at Triple Towers generations ago. She put the dozen chocolate crisp bars in her basket and perused the candy aisle further.

She had a few friends at her anger management group, and since Thursday would be their last meeting until the New Year, Shay wanted to have something for them too. She decided on chocolate oranges, another childhood favorite, and put several in her cart.

With her Army friendships just barely being rekindled, she didn't need to shop for anything there. So she checked out of the grocer, hoping her chocolate wouldn't melt while she continued down Main Street.

All she had left to shop for were the Royal brothers and their women. Shane had always been kind to her, never spoke without weighing everything, and worked hard. It was clear his brothers looked to him as the example, and he was willing to give it.

He and Robin had made the homestead an actual home again, and with that in mind, Shay wandered into a consignment store filled with booths. She went down one aisle and back up another before she found the perfect thing: A hand-carved sign depicting cows and grain towers in the distance that could be personalized. She could have the artist put Triple Towers Ranch on it, as well as Royal.

She picked up the card and dialed the number, hoping the carver would have time to make the sign before the holidays. He did, and she made arrangements to pick it up that weekend from the consignment shop.

Nothing else in the boutique caught her eye, and she went to the store next door. The shopping in Grape Seed Falls was sensational during the holidays, with lights strung from every doorway and rooftop, the scent of cinnamon hanging in the air, and music playing merrily inside every shop.

For the first time since she'd returned to town, Shay wanted to be there. She felt more at home walking down Main Street than she ever had. A swell of happiness hit her, and she smiled. Truly smiled at the positive emotions flowing through her.

She didn't know Dylan and Hazel as well, but she knew they'd be married soon and then be living in the tiny house until Dylan could build them something bigger. So what would they possibly like?

She knew Hazel had recently quit her job with Texas Parks & Wildlife, and operated a salon out of her house. Dylan was the quickest of the brothers to laugh, and they both generally seemed like they enjoyed having a good time.

"So a game," she announced to herself before turning into the toy shop. With the help of the owner's son, she found several card games that she could make a fun gift basket out of.

She picked up some socks and set her sights on finding a new pair of headphones for her father. He'd been complaining that his next-door neighbor listened to the television late into the night. He used to wear noise-cancelling headphones on the ranch so he could sleep at odd hours, and she found a pair in the electronics shop at the end of the street.

Satisfaction flowed through her that she'd gotten so much accomplished in just a few shops. But of course, the hardest person to shop for still remained on her list.

Austin.

She browsed shop after shop, and no ideas came.

She knew what she wanted to give him—something that she'd been missing these past several days. A warm hug. A quick kiss. Okay, maybe a long, deep kiss.

Her whole heart.

Her pulse twitched almost painfully in her chest, and she hurried back to her truck, the allure of shopping all the way gone.

She'd think of something for the cowboy who had snuck up on her like a thief in the night.

But Tuesday passed, and then Wednesday, and she still had no idea what to get for the man. She couldn't show up on Christmas Eve to the party without something for him. That would be too hurtful, and the last thing she wanted to do was damage Austin any more than she already had.

Thursday came, and her fingers twitched to text him all day. *Are you going to the meeting tonight?*

Want to ride together?

Take me for dinner after?

She sent him nothing, her emotions too raw and her embarrassment too hot. Besides the fact that she still didn't know if she had separated her craving for the ranch from her adoration of him.

And it wasn't fair to him to perpetuate a relationship where he wasn't the main prize.

"He *is* the main prize," she told herself as she drove down the lonely, two-lane highway back to town for the anger management meeting. She'd wrapped all the chocolate oranges in gold paper, with bright red ribbons crisscrossing them. They rode shotgun on the seat beside her, a poor substitute for the man she wished were sitting there.

She didn't see him sneak in the back of the meeting just before it started. He hadn't come, again. Her sharp disappointment would've normally turned to anger. Tonight, though, it simply stayed lodged in her chest as sadness.

Shawna got up to talk, and Shay tried to listen. She really did. But the words seemed to flow around her, muting as if they were underwater, and she couldn't grasp onto them. She was sure it was a great message, one Shay probably needed desperately in her life.

The meeting ended, and she passed out her gold-wrapped chocolate oranges, saying, "Merry Christmas," to the people she'd gotten to know. She held on extra tight to Shawna, who drew her back and looked deep into her eyes.

"What's wrong, Shay?"

"Oh, you know." Shay tried to laugh, but it came out strangled. At least she didn't have any tears threatening to spill down her face.

"No, I don't know." Shawna glanced around the room, which was mostly empty except for two women putting away the chairs. "How about we go for coffee?"

"Make it hot chocolate and I'm there."

Shawna gave her a friendly smile and stepped back. "Hot chocolate it is. C'mon, darlin'. I'll drive."

Shay didn't have it in her to argue, and she did want to talk to someone. She couldn't say anything to her father, and she didn't have girlfriends she spent hours gossiping with. As a general rule, Shay didn't gossip at all, which made having female relationships a little harder than she deemed necessary.

She let Shawna fill the silence on the short drive over to the ice cream shop, which surprisingly, served the best hot chocolate in town. A teenager filled their cups and passed the steaming treat over to them. Shawna waited until she'd sipped several times before she finally relaxed.

"So, tell me what's going on."

"I broke up with my boyfriend." Shay sounded miserable, even to her own ears.

"Why?"

"It's complicated." She ran her hands through her hair and down her face. "I'm basically a great big mess, and I don't know how I feel."

Shawna nodded, sipped, watched. It was almost unnerving how she expected Shay to talk, and Shay found herself covering the silence now.

"We work out on the ranch together. He actually bought the ranch from my dad. Okay, not just him, but him and his brothers. He asked me to dance at his brother's wedding, and I wouldn't, because I was just so mad, you know?"

"Losing the ranch was very difficult for you," Shawna said.

Shay had told her that before, and it wasn't like it was a secret anyway. "Yeah. And here's this man, and he's like, perfect almost—except for his own daddy issues, some anger, and a little bit of jealousy. Oh, and the fact that he doesn't like mushrooms, which obviously make an omelet and should be included in every soup recipe."

She sighed, her memory bank overflowing at the happenings of the past month. "But then he's hardworking too. And sweet. And kind. And he likes me. Like really likes me, and I don't know what to do with that, because I don't have men who are interested in me."

"Why's that?"

"Oh, you know. I'm too prickly. I intimidate them. I can fix a helicopter faster than them. That kind of thing."

"Mm." Shawna drained the last of her hot chocolate and ordered more, this time with a caramel swirl in it. When she returned to the table, she asked, "And you don't think it's because you put off the vibe that you're unavailable? That a man better not ask, because you'll just say no?"

Shay blinked and stared at Shawna. "Is that the vibe I put off?"

"What do you think?"

She thought about it, and Shay didn't like at all that she had to say, "Yeah, that's probably the vibe I put off."

"And somehow this man penetrated that?"

Oh, Austin had definitely broken through her external barriers. Her internal ones too. She sighed. "Yeah."

"You sound like you really like him."

"I do."

"Then what's the problem?"

"I'm worried that I'm only dating him so I can get some of the ranch back." There, she'd said it. Right out loud to another person.

To Shawna's credit, she barely reacted. She blinked and stood when the teen called her name for her second round of hot chocolate. When she returned to the table, she said, "Is that really true? You don't strike me as the kind of woman who would go to all the trouble of dating just to get thirty percent of a ranch."

Shay ducked her head, her own drink growing colder by the minute. "I'd get to stay there," she said quietly. "And my job wouldn't be in question. And it would practically be like I owned the ranch. I've seen how the brothers work together."

She shook her head now, trying to dislodge the uncomfortable thoughts. "I've already requested to meet with his brother after the holidays. Talk to him about...well, perhaps it's time I move on."

Shawna's eyes locked onto hers. "You'd leave the ranch? Don't you have a guarantee of working there until next summer?"

Shay nodded. "Yeah, but...." She needed to know she wasn't using Austin in any way related to the ranch.

"Okay, listen." Shawna set down her hot chocolate. "Just answer a couple of questions. Now, I know you don't like them—a" She flashed a smile, her eyes kind and lit from within. "But just the first thing that comes to mind, okay?"

"Okay."

"Do you wish you still had the ranch?"

"Yes, of course."

"Do you like this man enough to be thinking about marriage?"

"Yes." Shay's answer was much quieter now.

"Would you give up the ranch to be with him?"

"Yes."

Shawna sat back, beaming as she lifted her cup. "There you go."

"There you go? What just happened?"

"You, Shay, just said you're in love with Austin Royal, and that you'd *give—up* your ranch to be *with—him*." Shawna pointed with each enunciated word. "Think about that for a minute. Just think about it."

Shay's mind whirred, blurred, blended, whipped around, each thought flying faster than the last. "So...."

"So you're in love with him. The ranch is non-essential. You can take it or leave it. But Austin? You need him."

"I need him." Shay numbly lifted her eyes to meet her friend's. "How did you know it was Austin Royal?"

"Oh, honey. All the single ladies in town know when a handsome bachelor gets taken off the market." She laughed, her nearly black curls bouncing with the movement. "Now, come on. If I stay here much longer, I'll get another one of these and won't be able to fit into my jeans tomorrow." She stood with all the grace and elegance of a princess, and Shay grabbed onto her and hugged her.

"Thank you," she whispered.

"Oh, you did all the work, darlin'. Now you better figure out how to get that man back."

CHAPTER TWENTY-ONE

Somehow, Austin managed to sleep in his own house without getting up and standing on the back deck, his eyes trained on Shay's front door like a creeper. He managed to get Christmas presents for the ranch hands, his brothers, Robin and Hazel, his mother *and* her boyfriend, his father, and everyone at Grape Seed Ranch.

And somehow, miraculously, he also got Shane and Dylan to agree to invite their father for Christmas. Shane's stipulation was that their dad had to sleep at Austin's, and Dylan's condition was that their mother had to give her consent too.

Austin called her on Tuesday evening while he sat in the truck, the Christmas presents he'd spent the afternoon buying filling the cab beside him. "Hey, Ma," he said when she answered. Her voice made everything in his life softer. "So I've got somethin' to ask you, and it's okay for you to say no."

Dylan had told Austin he had to allow their mom to say no. Not be mad about it. Honor it.

"All right," she said. "Go on then."

"It's about Dad," Austin started. "I know you're comin' for Christmas with Barry, and that's still all good and fine. I'm not sure if you heard about Dad and Joanna, but she left, and well, I thought it would be nice if he had somewhere to go for Christmas where he wouldn't be alone."

He pressed his eyes closed, a steady prayer streaming through his mind. "And he'd stay with me," Austin added. "So you and Barry would be with Shane and Robin. Dad would be with me, and I don't live in the homestead anymore."

His mother still didn't say anything, and Austin's hopes deflated. "It's okay to say no," he reminded her.

"I'm not going to say no," she finally said. "I made my peace with your dad a long time ago, and no one should be alone on Christmas."

"Yeah?" Austin asked.

"Of course." She sounded perfectly pleasant, but Austin hoped he hadn't caused her any stress.

"Thanks, Mom."

"You're a good boy, Austin. You've always had the softest heart."

Austin suddenly felt shaky, and he didn't know what to say. He felt like he didn't have a heart at all, that maybe he'd given it to Shay and was waiting for her to bring it back.

"We got a Christmas tree put up last night," he said. "And the whole ranch is lit up. You're gonna love it."

"I'm sure I will."

"See you soon, then."

"Thursday."

Austin hung up, his emotions ping-ponging around inside him, bouncing off each other and combining into dangerous concoctions. He didn't know what to do with them, so he picked up his phone and did something he knew how to do.

He called his dad and invited him to the Christmas festivities on the ranch.

"AND YOU INVITED SHAY, RIGHT?" AUSTIN STOOD NEXT TO Shane in the kitchen of the homestead, pouring a cup of coffee while his brother scrambled eggs. A lot of eggs. Robin's mother had arrived last night, and Barry and Mom had arrived on Thursday night. Hazel was coming out for breakfast before the Sunday Christmas service, and even Dad said he'd come over for something to eat.

"I invited all the ranch hands," Shane said evenly, just like he had the other five times Austin had asked. "She has not specifically confirmed she'll be comin'. She's welcome, as I told her, whether she RSVPs or not." He nodded toward the saltshaker. "Give that a spin around the pan."

Austin did as his brother instructed, wishing he knew for certain if he was going to see Shay that day or not. It was Christmas Eve. She shouldn't be alone, and her father had confirmed his attendance at the gift exchange later that evening, as well as Christmas Dinner the following day. What would Shay do —where would she go—if she didn't join them?

He couldn't stand the thought of her being by herself, or even going to someone else's house. He wanted her here, beside him, as they opened gifts and sang carols and read the story of the Savior's birth from the Bible.

There were only eight people for the family breakfast before church, but there would be twenty-one for the gift exchange. Twenty-two if Shay came. Plenty of others for her to hide behind. He probably wouldn't even have to talk to her if she did come.

"Let's eat," Shane said, setting the hot pan on the hot pad on the counter. He glanced around, and Austin did too. Their dad hadn't come. Disappointment cut through Austin, but he brushed it off. His dad wasn't going to influence how he felt anymore. He was a grown man, and he'd been invited to the family breakfast. If he chose not to come, that was on him.

Robin said grace, and everyone put eggs, French toast, and sausage on their plates. It was a happy, bubbly atmosphere, and Austin basked in the warmth of it. He loved his family, and he

couldn't think of anywhere he'd rather be in that moment. Sure, he
wanted Shay there with him, to show her that there were families
that rebuilt after tragedy. That she had a place on this ranch even
if she didn't own it.

After cleaning up, he rode with his mom and Barry into town.
Barry was a nice guy—a retired dentist who'd lost all his hair a long
time ago. He told stories of his own grown children, and Austin
had learned that his wife had died about five years ago.

The way his mother glowed meant she was obviously smitten
by Barry, and Austin had to admit he couldn't find anything to
dislike. Contentment spread through him. His mom deserved to
be happy, to be cherished, to have someone to spend her life with
that wouldn't ruin her.

Once at the church, they joined the streams of people heading
inside. He looked around for Shay but couldn't see her. There were
so many people—and more still coming in—the balcony had been
opened. She literally could've been right in front of him and Austin
wouldn't have seen her.

He managed to squeeze himself against the wall, turning side-
ways to make room for everyone else along the row. Pastor Gifford
looked like someone had put a light bulb in his mouth and turned
him on. He glowed as he spoke about the Savior and His birth,
encouraged everyone to take the Christmas spirit with them
throughout the year, and ended early so "folks can spend time with
their families."

Austin wanted to take this joyful, peaceful feeling and bottle it
up. Drink it every time he felt himself slipping into a bad mood or
getting frustrated with someone or something. *How can I do that?*

"You comin'?"

He glanced up to see Shane waiting for him behind the bench,
and Austin scrambled to his feet. "Yeah, comin'."

"You looked lost there." Shane pinned him with that parental
older brother look Austin didn't appreciate.

"I'm fine."

"Why don't you just go talk to Shay?" They inched toward the exit, the crowd making the escape slow and tedious. "See if she's coming tonight. Put yourself out of your misery."

"I could, I guess." Austin stuffed his hands in his pockets and trained his feet on the floor in front of him. "I just don't want to… crowd her. You know? She said she needed time."

"It's been almost two weeks."

"I know how long it's been." Every day, every hour, every second was agony. A moment passed where Austin couldn't breathe, and then his involuntary functions fired again.

"Think about it." Shane separated from him once they went outside, and Austin headed back to his mom's car alone.

Back at the ranch, his mother put everyone to work hanging up a stocking for every ranch hand and everyone who was coming. This was a Royal family tradition, one she'd done on their ranch growing up. Everyone got gifts on Christmas Eve, even the seasonal worker they'd hired the week before.

Once the stockings were all hung, his mother went around humming holiday hymns as she sifted through her bag of socks to find the right pair for the person. She always gave socks on Christmas Eve, saying everyone always needed a new pair of socks.

Throughout the afternoon, everyone managed to bring their gifts and fill the stockings for the ranch hands. Austin had something for Shay, but he didn't dare put it in her stocking for everyone to see.

It was too personal, and it would probably make her mad now that they weren't dating anymore. She didn't wear much jewelry, and he couldn't very well give her something so impersonal as a gift card to the Soup Kitchen. He'd seen a few mementoes around her house that testified of her love of the ranch and her love of her parents, and he'd taken the photo of her he'd found and had it professionally framed.

Shay was probably eight in the picture, and her mother's illness and subsequent death still a decade away. She'd clearly won something, as Austin had noticed a ribbon pinned to her shirt that he hadn't seen the first time he'd found the photo.

The frame was silver—Shay's preferred metal color—and adored with flowers along the bottom. A rectangle for engraving was there, and Austin had chosen to put the word FAMILY there.

Family was important to Shay. It was what had driven her from the ranch and brought her back. Austin desperately wanted her to feel like part of the family on this ranch, so with only thirty minutes to go until the gift exchange would start, he put his cowboy hat on and caught his brother's eye.

"I'll be back."

"Good luck," Shane said, nothing else needed.

Austin stepped out through the back door so he wouldn't have to pass his mother and answer any questions.

He'd rounded the corner of the house and taken four strides when two German shepherds came into view. They saw him and bounded forward, their master down the road a bit and walking with hesitant steps.

"Shay." The word breathed out of his mouth, but she lifted her head as if she'd heard him. Of course she couldn't. She was much too far away for that.

But she'd seen him now, and she'd stopped walking altogether. She wore a pair of jeans and a green blouse the exact shade of Christmas. Her cowgirl hat sat on her head perfectly, and she was wearing her glasses today. He wasn't sure if that was because her eyes hurt, or she was expecting to cry that day, or something else entirely.

A wet nose touched his hand, and he turned his attention to her dogs. "Hey, Lizzy." Austin scrubbed one dog's head and then the next. "Molly. What've you guys been doin', huh?" He gave them a good pat each then looked back at Shay. She carried a bag clearly laden with gifts, and he wondered what she'd have for him.

He stood and strode toward her, suddenly wanting to exchange gifts in private. The picture frame was still at his house—along with his father.

"Hey." He stopped a few paces from her. "I have something for you at my place. I was just goin' to get it." Not really true, but not entirely false either. "I was just going to drop it by, since I wasn't sure if you were coming this evening or not."

She looked at him with those beautiful caramel-coffee eyes. "I have something for you at my cabin too. I...I didn't want to give it to you in front of everyone."

His heart grew wings and lifted into the air, soaring and flying through the clouds. She had a gift for him. Not only that, but a gift she didn't want to give him in public.

"Should we maybe do our exchange now? Or do you want to wait until after?"

"Now's fine." She looked down at the bag she was carrying. "This is chocolate though. Should I put it in the house so it doesn't melt?"

Though the temperatures weren't hitting record highs, the sun was warm today. "Sure," Austin said, reaching for the bag. "I'll take it and be right back."

She relinquished the bag to him, and he hurried to put it in the kitchen, near panic that she'd be gone when he returned. He'd felt like this before, and he hated that he didn't trust her enough to know she'd be standing in the middle of the road, right where he left her.

It felt natural to reach for her hand, pick up right where they left off almost two weeks ago. To keep himself from doing exactly that, he put his hands in his pockets and added a couple of feet of distance between them as they walked back the way she'd come.

An engine filled the air, and Austin searched for the source of it, finding his father's truck easily. He slowed to a stop, the window already down. "I'm just going over for the gift exchange."

"Right," Austin said. "I left something at my place. We're going to get it, and then we'll be right there."

His father flicked his gaze to Shay and back to Austin. "All right." He continued down the road, and Austin thought it strange he'd driven. It was probably three or four blocks—a ten-minute walk—and the weather was gorgeous.

"I want to see your new place," she said when they reached the crossroads. "So let me grab your gift, and I'll meet you over there. Okay?" She didn't wait for him to answer before she continued east and he had no choice but to go north.

His house smelled muskier than usual, and he hurried to open a window to air the place out. Shay arrived only a few minutes later, and her timid knock on the front door sent his pulse into palpitations.

He opened the door to find her holding a large sugar cookie in the shape of a heart. It had been decorated with soft pink frosting and it had his name elegantly piped onto the front. The clear cellophane bag had been tied with a red ribbon.

Shay held it up by the top of the bag so that it dangled between them. "I'm giving you my heart."

Austin's throat felt so narrow, and his mind so soft. He looked at the cookie and then Shay, searching searching searching for an answer. He didn't dare hope, and yet that was the dominant emotion cascading through him like river rapids.

"What does—I mean—?"

"I'm in love with you, Austin Royal. And while it terrifies me to no end, I've decided I trust you." She shook the bag slightly. "I spent all morning making this so that it was just right. You better take it—and don't break it."

He wasn't sure if she was literally talking about the heart-shaped cookie, or her actual heart. All he could hear was *I'm in love with you, Austin Royal.*

He took the cookie, focusing on it until he could think straight. I'm in love with you, Austin Royal.

"Does this mean you want me more than the ranch?"

"I've always wanted you more than the ranch," she said.

He looked up at her, that joy and peace flooding him when he saw how sincere she was. Her hands shook the teensiest bit as she reached for him, and Austin drew her securely into his arms.

"Ah, there you are," he breathed. "You fit so great right here, close to me."

"I've missed you," she whispered. "I'm sorry."

"Nothing to be sorry about." He drew back, gazed down at her, and smiled. "Okay? Not one thing."

"I'll still need time."

"I won't break your heart."

Her smile was a little wobbly, but she nodded.

"I won't," he repeated. "Because I'm in love with you too."

CHAPTER TWENTY-TWO

Shay felt at home in Austin's cabin, inside his embrace, with his beautiful words filling her ears. He loved her.

And when he kissed her, she could feel it in the tenderness of his touch. Sense it in the way his lips trembled slightly against hers before capturing them more firmly. She believed it in the way he pressed her closer to him, and gave as much as he took.

He pulled away and said, "All I want for Christmas, ever, is you." It should've been cheesy, a line from a song. But he was serious, his blue eyes burning like the hottest part of a fire.

Then he asked, "Can I really not eat that cookie?"

She sucked in a breath and then giggled, the sound turning into a full laugh a few moments later. "Yeah, you can eat it."

"Let me give you your present first." He stepped away from her, and she moved all the way into his cabin. He'd bought a set of modern black couches that somehow fit in the rustic cabin. A small dining room table sat in the far corner, with the kitchen opposite it, with three bright blue barstools at the counter.

He picked something up off the table and turned back to her, hiding it behind him. "I didn't wrap it. I wasn't sure when I'd give it to you."

"You just said you were going to drop it off."

"Yeah, well, I wasn't."

"I probably would've eaten that heart for breakfast," she admitted. "Though I ate about five cookies today already. I've been kind of nervous."

He nodded, like her nervousness was normal. "Me too. I just wasn't sure if you were coming or not." He stepped forward, his voice soft when he added, "I'm glad you came."

"Me too." Shay really wanted to see what he had behind his back, so she settled onto the loveseat and waited.

"This might not mean much," he said, joining her but keeping the gift hidden. "But when I saw it, I thought it was perfect. And that you'd want it." He brought his hands out from behind him to reveal a silver picture frame.

She took it from him, her eyes locked onto the trio the photograph depicted. Tears touched her eyes when she saw the radiant smiles on her parents' faces. On her own face.

"When was that?" he asked. "I think you're about eight."

"I'm nine," she said. "And I've just won the jump roping contest at school." She glanced up at him, not even caring that she was about to cry. "See that ribbon? First place in the fourth grade Olympics. I was so happy, and my parents took me out to dinner to celebrate. We took this just before we left."

"That's what I saw in it," he said. "Happiness. Family. Joy. Faith. It seemed like everything your childhood was, before your mother died."

Shay traced her finger over her face, which held more happiness than she'd felt in a long time. "It was all of those things."

"My brothers and I...." He cleared his throat. "We want all of that for this ranch again. They have someone to help them build it. But I need you."

I need you.

I love you.

Shay wiped her eyes and looked at Austin, right into the depths of his eyes, all the way into his soul. And she let him all the way into her life, her mind, her soul too. "All right."

He drew her into his embrace again, the picture getting smashed between them as he kissed her like a man in love. Shay had never been kissed like that, and she wanted to hold onto every last moment of it.

Finally, she said, "Your phone has gone off three times. Everyone is probably wondering where you are."

He jolted and pulled his phone from his back pocket. "Shoot. We're late. C'mon." He extended his hand to her, and Shay had never been happier to slide her fingers through his. He called his brother as they descended the steps and said, "Yeah, those are Shay's. Can you distribute them? We're walking back now. Be there in a few minutes."

He hung up. "Dylan's handing out your gifts. They'll wait for us. I guess a couple of the ranch hands haven't come in from their chores yet either."

She kept her hand firmly in his as they walked back, and when he led her up the front steps and into the house, Shay finally felt like she was coming home.

The air smelled like pine trees and sugar, and the sight of thirty stockings hung at various heights along the walls met her eyes. She pulled in a breath and pressed one hand over her chest.

"This is beautiful," she said, gaping at the lit Christmas tree, with pure white lights and dozens of multi-colored ornaments. Another couch had been brought into the room, along with a piano bench and lots of chairs.

Austin's mother stood from one of the chairs, her eyes taking in everything between Shay and Austin with a single sweep. A smile graced her face, and she said, "Hello, Shay, dear," before giving Shay a hug.

Shay held on tight, knowing she should let go of the woman before things became too awkward. But she smelled just like Shay's mother had, and she hadn't hugged her mother in so, so long. Unexpected tears burned in her eyes and Shay pulled back to look at Alex. "Merry Christmas." Her voice was little more than a whisper.

"To you too." Alex stepped back and indicated a very tall, very bald man. "This is my boyfriend, Barry Dalton. Barry, this is Austin's girlfriend, Shayleigh Hatch."

Pleasantries were exchanged and the front door opened again, and more ranch hands entered the house.

"All right," Shane called, and more people entered from the kitchen. Somehow, they all piled into the living room, and every chair got taken. She met the piercing blue eyes of Austin's father, a man she hadn't met yet, but he settled near the entryway to the kitchen, out of the way of everyone.

"Welcome to our annual Christmas Eve gift exchange." Shane smiled at everyone like he was a six-year-old looking at Santa himself. "We've got appetizers and finger foods in the kitchen, but we'll do the gifts first."

"And dinner tomorrow is at noon," Dylan said. "My mom is makin' her famous brown sugar spiced ham, and everyone is invited if you're not goin' to visit family or anything." He looked at Austin, who stood.

"So when we were boys, my mother would hang stockings for everyone on the ranch. She'd add little gifts to them the entire month of December and on Christmas Eve, we'd all gather to open everything inside. So, we wanted to recreate that here at our own ranch, since the one we used to have was...lost." He swept his eyes past his father, and his face turned the slightest bit pink.

"So anyway. You all have a stocking here. We'll pass them out, and you can start unpacking them." He moved to the one closest to him and unpinned it from the wall. He walked over to Oaker and handed it to him.

Giddiness paraded through her, her anticipation high, as she waited for her stocking to be delivered. Austin kept hers in his hand until the very end, then he sat down beside her and handed it over. He flashed her a sexy, handsome smile and then started rummaging through his own presents.

People laughed, offered gratitude, and started eating some of the treats they'd received. Shay pulled out chocolates, peppermint bark, and a sucker with a scorpion in it. She got socks, a bag of hard suckers, and gloves. Each little gift was nothing all that special. They had her name on them and who they were from.

As she looked around the room, a rush of peace and gratitude filled her. This was what Triple Towers Ranch was meant to be. A gathering place for anyone and everyone who came here. A place of refuge from the storms of life. Love, laughter, joy.

She knew she never could've brought that to this ranch. But the Royal brothers could. They already had. They'd made a family out of the ranch in just six short months.

And while she'd decided several days ago to try and get Austin back in her life, she still wasn't one hundred percent sure her reasons were pure.

But she knew now. Looking around at all the smiles, listening to the laughter, and basking in the joy, she knew that Triple Towers Ranch was meant to be theirs. She could only hope and pray that she got to stay here for as long as possible, in whatever capacity the Lord deemed right for her.

THE FOLLOWING DAY, SHAY WOKE WITH THE FIRST RAYS OF dawn. Christmas Day always felt different, for a reason Shay couldn't quite name. But she felt loved in that moment, and she closed her eyes again and offered a prayer of gratitude for the feeling.

Shane had declared that they were doing just minimal chores that day to keep everything alive, so she took her time getting ready. She didn't work directly with animals, but Austin did, and she knew she'd find him in the hen houses, herding the chickens out to the yard so he could feed them.

Sure enough, he stood there, clucking along with his birds, a fondness in his eyes for the fowl that she certainly didn't understand.

"Morning." She leaned against the fence and watched one particularly plump chicken strut around, pecking the ground every other step.

"Hey, beautiful." He walked through the feathers and kissed her. "Did you sleep well?" After the gift exchange, she'd snacked on deviled eggs, drunk hot chocolate, and eaten more than her fair share of the caramel popcorn. Austin had stuck by her side all night and insisted on walking her home.

He'd kissed her under the light of the moon, and Shay had once again felt the love and passion he seemed to have for her.

"Well enough," she said. "Took me forever to get going today."

"I can see that. It's almost nine, and you're just now showin' up." He gave her a grin and went back to his work. "Of course, I've been out here for two hours and I'm still not done. So."

She detected something in his voice. "Oh, yeah? Don't want to go home?"

"My dad's there." He shrugged. "He's fine. I didn't want him to be alone on Christmas."

"Well, I have to go pick mine up in an hour or so. You're welcome to ride along if you're not needed in the food prep."

"Is that a joke?" He grinned at her. "You think I can't cook."

"I know you can't cook." She laughed and reached back to start braiding her hair. "But maybe they need you to set the table or put out extra chairs."

"I can ride along," he said, his voice a little too casual.

Shay giggled again. "All right, then. I'm gonna take Lizzy and Molly out for a bit. Get them nice and tired so they don't bark during dinner."

"Come pick me up when you're ready to go."

She waved at him, then whistled at her dogs to come with her. She walked down the road, throwing a ball the shepherds fought over every time. After an hour out in the fields with them, she put them in the back of her truck and started to climb in the cab.

But a card and a black box the size of a deck of cards stopped her. Her heart pounded furiously in her chest, and her fingers shook as she reached for the card.

It was a Christmas card, with a beautiful, watercolored tree on the front. Gold lettering said Merry Christmas in swirling, cursive font, and Austin's chicken scratch had been penned on the inside.

I know this might not be traditional, but I guess we're not very traditional around these parts. I love you, Shay. I'm hoping that by next Christmas you'll be my wife.

Love, Austin

Shay pushed her breath out in a steady stream. "Is this a proposal?" she asked the empty air around her.

"Yes."

She spun to find Austin loitering near the front of the truck. She dropped the card, everything that was happening coming at her from all sides. Scrambling to pick it up, she faced him, her mouth dry.

"You're asking me to marry you?"

"Yes, ma'am." He'd cleaned up nicely and now wore clean jeans with a bright green sweater with Christmas lights embroidered on it. She almost started laughing, and he glanced down at his chest.

"So my mother makes us wear an ugly Christmas sweater every year." He grinned and shrugged one shoulder. "It makes her happy."

Adoration flowed through Shay, but she still couldn't quite wrap her head around the card she held and the box she hadn't opened yet.

"So I know you said you needed time," he said, crowding into the space between the open door and the truck. He picked up the black box. "A year's a long time, Shay. Maybe we can get married at Christmastime, next year."

He looked at her, his eyes barely meeting hers from under the brim of his cowboy hat. "You'd make me the happiest man in Texas if you said yes." He cracked open the box to reveal a beautiful, brilliant diamond. Nothing huge or fancy. Just something classic. Something perfect.

Shay's pulse clamored in her chest. She met Austin's eye, and all the nerves, all the anxiety, all the worry, left her body in one fluid rush of energy.

"Yes," she said.

He whooped, grabbed her around the waist, and twirled her away from the truck and onto the sparse front lawn. "Yes?"

"Yes." She laughed this time, and her hands continued to shake like brittle leaves in an autumn wind as he slid the engagement ring onto her left ring finger.

"I love you, Shay." He touched his nose to hers, sobering the moment. "I've loved you for a long time."

"I love you too, cowboy." She tilted her head back to align her mouth with his and kissed her fiancé.

The End

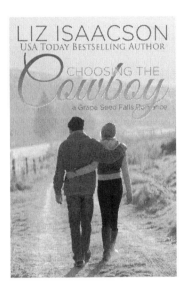
A spinoff from the #1 bestselling Three Rivers Ranch Romance novels, also by USA Today bestselling author Liz Isaacson.

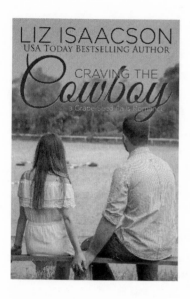

Craving the Cowboy (Book 2): Dwayne Carver is set to inherit his family's ranch in the heart of Texas Hill Country, and in order to keep up with his ranch duties and fulfill his dreams of owning a horse farm, he hires top trainer Felicity Lightburne. They get along great, and she can envision herself on this new farm—at least until her mother falls ill and she has to return to help her. Can Dwayne and Felicity work through their differences to find their happily-ever-after?

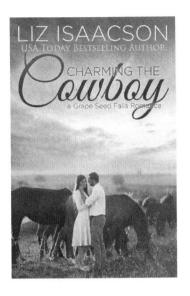

Charming the Cowboy (Book 3): Third grade teacher Heather Carver has had her eye on Levi Rhodes for a couple of years now, but he seems to be blind to her attempts to charm him. When she breaks her arm while on his horse ranch, Heather infiltrates Levi's life in ways he's never thought of, and his strict anti-female stance slips. Will Heather heal his emotional scars and he care for her physical ones so they can have a real relationship?

Courting the Cowboy (Book 4): Frustrated with the cowboy-only dating scene in Grape Seed Falls, May Sotheby joins Texas-Faithful.com, hoping to find her soul mate without having to relo-cate--or deal with cowboy hats and boots. She has no idea that Kurt Pemberton, foreman at Grape Seed Ranch, is the man she starts communicating with... Will May be able to follow her heart and get Kurt to forgive her so they can be together?

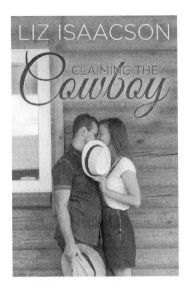

Claiming the Cowboy, Royal Brothers Book 1 (Grape Seed Falls Romance Book 5): Unwilling to be tied down, farrier Robin Cook has managed to pack her entire life into a two-hundred-and-eighty square-foot house, and that includes her Yorkie. Cowboy and co-foreman, Shane Royal has had his heart set on Robin for three years, even though she flat-out turned him down the last time he asked her to dinner. But she's back at Grape Seed Ranch for five weeks as she works her horseshoeing magic, and he's still interested, despite a bitter life lesson that left a bad taste for marriage in his mouth.

Robin's interested in him too. But can she find room for Shane in her tiny house--and can he take a chance on her with his tired heart?

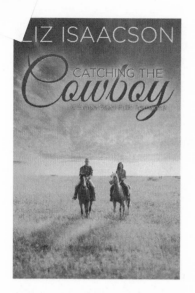

Catching the Cowboy, Royal Brothers Book 2 (Grape Seed Falls Romance Book 6): Dylan Royal is good at two things: whistling and caring for cattle. When his cows are being attacked by an unknown wild animal, he calls Texas Parks & Wildlife for help. He wasn't expecting a beautiful mammologist to show up, all flirty and fun and everything Dylan didn't know he wanted in his life.

Hazel Brewster has gone on more first dates than anyone in Grape Seed Falls, and she thinks maybe Dylan deserves a second... Can they find their way through wild animals, huge life changes, and their emotional pasts to find their forever future?

Cheering the Cowboy, Royal Brothers Book 3 (Grape Seed Falls Romance Book 7): Austin Royal loves his life on his new ranch with his brothers. But he doesn't love that Shayleigh Hatch came with the property, nor that he has to take the blame for the fact that he now owns her childhood ranch. They rarely have a conversation that doesn't leave him furious and frustrated-- and yet he's still attracted to Shay in a strange, new way.

Shay inexplicably likes him too, which utterly confuses and angers her. As they work to make this Christmas the best the Triple Towers Ranch has ever seen, can they also navigate through their rocky relationship to smoother waters?

BOOKS IN THE STEEPLE RIDGE ROMANCE SERIES:

Starting Over at Steeple Ridge: Steeple Ridge Romance (Book 1): Tucker Jenkins has had enough of tall buildings, traffic, and has traded in his technology firm in New York City for Steeple Ridge Horse Farm in rural Vermont. Missy Marino has worked at the farm since she was a teen, and she's always dreamed of owning it. But her ex-husband left her with a truckload of debt, making her fantasies of owning the farm unfulfilled. Tucker didn't come to the country to find a new wife, but he supposes a woman could help him start over in Steeple Ridge. Will Tucker and Missy be able to navigate the shaky ground between them to find a new beginning?

Finding Love at Steeple Ridge: A Butters Brothers Novel, Steeple Ridge Romance (Book 2): Ben Buttars is the youngest of the four Buttars brothers who come to Steeple Ridge Farm, and he finally feels like he's landed somewhere he can make a life for himself. Reagan Cantwell is a decade older than Ben and the recreational direction for the town of Island Park. Though Ben is young, he knows what he wants—and that's Rae. Can she figure out how to put what matters most in her life—family and faith—above her job before she loses Ben?

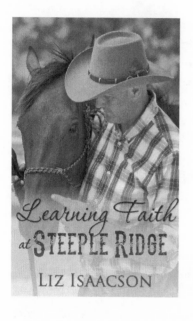

Learning Faith at Steeple Ridge: A Butters Brothers Novel, Steeple Ridge Romance (Book 3): Sam Buttars has spent the last decade making sure he and his brothers stay together. They've been at Steeple Ridge for a while now, but with the youngest married and happy, the siren's call to return to his parents' farm in Wyoming is loud in Sam's ears. He'd just go if it weren't for beautiful Bonnie Sherman, who roped his heart the first time he saw her. Do Sam and Bonnie have the faith to find comfort in each other instead of in the people who've already passed?

Kissing Santa at STEEPLE RIDGE

LIZ ISAACSON

Learning Faith at Steeple Ridge: A Butters Brothers Novel, Steeple Ridge Romance (Book 4): Logan Buttars has always been good-natured and happy-go-lucky. After watching two of his brothers settle down, he recognizes a void in his life he didn't know about. Veterinarian Layla Guyman has appreciated Logan's friendship and easy way with animals when he comes into the clinic to get the service dogs. But with his future at Steeple Ridge in the balance, she's not sure a relationship with him is worth the risk. Can she rely on her faith and employ patience to tame Logan's wild heart?

Learning Faith at Steeple Ridge: A Butters Brothers Novel, Steeple Ridge Romance (Book 5): Darren Buttars is cool, collected, and quiet—and utterly devastated when his girlfriend of nine months, Farrah Irvine, breaks up with him because he wanted her to ride her horse in a parade. But Farrah doesn't ride anymore, a fact she made very clear to Darren. She returned to her childhood home with so much baggage, she doesn't know where to start with the unpacking. Darren's the only Buttars brother who isn't married, and he wants to make Island Park his permanent home—with Farrah. Can they find their way through the heartache to achieve a happily-ever-after together?

BOOKS IN THE GOLD VALLEY ROMANCE SERIES:

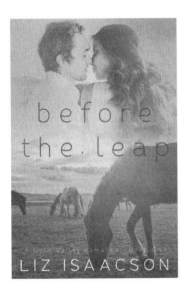

Before the Leap: A Gold Valley Romance (Book 1): Jace Lovell only has one thing left after his fiancé abandons him at the altar: his job at Horseshoe Home Ranch. Belle Edmunds is back in Gold Valley and she's desperate to build a portfolio that she can use to start her own firm in Montana. Jace isn't anywhere near forgiving his fiancé, and he's not sure he's ready for a new relationship with someone as fiery and beautiful as Belle. Can she employ her patience while he figures out how to forgive so they can find their own brand of happily-ever-after?

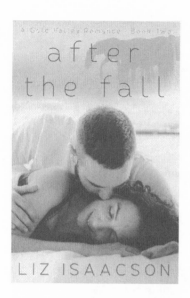

After the Fall: A Gold Valley Romance (Book 2): Professional snowboarder Sterling Maughan has sequestered himself in his family's cabin in the exclusive mountain community above Gold Valley, Montana after a devastating fall that ended his career. Norah Watson cleans Sterling's cabin and the more time they spend together, the more Sterling is interested in all things Norah. As his body heals, so does his faith. Will Norah be able to trust Sterling so they can have a chance at true love?

Through the Mist: A Gold Valley Romance (Book 3): Landon Edmunds has been a cowboy his whole life. An accident five years ago ended his successful rodeo career, and now he's looking to start a horse ranch--and he's looking outside of Montana. Which would be great if God hadn't brought Megan Palmer back to Gold Valley right when Landon is looking to leave. Megan and Landon work together well, and as sparks fly, she's sure God brought her back to Gold Valley so she could find her happily ever after. Through serious discussion and prayer, can Landon and Megan find their future together?

Be sure to check out the spinoff series, the Brush Creek Brides romances after you read THROUGH THE MIST. Start with A WEDDING FOR THE WIDOWER.

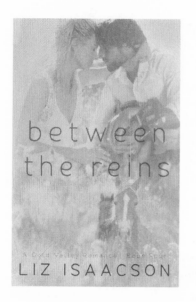

between the reins

A Gold Valley Romance · Book Four

LIZ ISAACSON

Between the Reins: A Gold Valley Romance (Book 4): Twelve years ago, Owen Carr left Gold Valley—and his long-time girlfriend—in favor of a country music career in Nashville. Married and divorced, Natalie teaches ballet at the dance studio in Gold Valley, but she never auditioned for the professional company the way she dreamed of doing. With Owen back, she realizes all the opportunities she missed out on when he left all those years ago—including a future with him. Can they mend broken bridges in order to have a second chance at love?

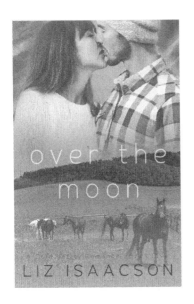

Over the Moon: A Gold Valley Romance (Book 5): Caleb Chamberlain has spent the last five years recovering from a horrible breakup, his alcoholism that stemmed from it, and the car accident that left him hospitalized. He's finally on the right track in his life—until Holly Gray, his twin brother's ex-fiance mistakes him for Nathan. Holly's back in Gold Valley to get the required veterinarian hours to apply for her graduate program. When the herd at Horseshoe Home comes down with pneumonia, Caleb and Holly are forced to work together in close quarters. Holly's over Nathan, but she hasn't forgiven him—or the woman she believes broke up their relationship. Can Caleb and Holly navigate such a rough past to find their happily-ever-after?

Journey to Steeple Ridge Farm with Holly—and fall in love with the cowboys there in the Steeple Ridge Romance series! Start with STARTING OVER AT STEEPLE RIDGE.

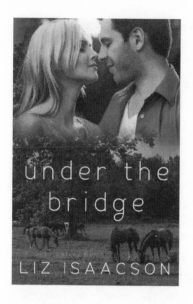

Under the Bridge: A Gold Valley Romance (Book 6): Ty Barker has been dancing through the last thirty years of his life-- and he's suddenly realized he's alone. River Lee Whitely is back in Gold Valley with her two little girls after a divorce that's left deep scars. She has a job at Silver Creek that requires her to be able to ride a horse, and she nearly tramples Ty at her first lesson. That's just fine by him, because River Lee is the girl Ty has never gotten over. Ty realizes River Lee needs time to settle into her new job, her new home, her new life as a single parent, but going slow has never been his style. But for River Lee, can Ty take the necessary steps to keep her in his life?

Up on the Housetop: A Gold Valley Romance (Book 7): Archer Bailey has already lost one job to Emersyn Enders, so he deliberately doesn't tell her about the cowhand job up at Horseshoe Home Ranch. Emery's temporary job is ending, but her obligations to her physically disabled sister aren't. As Archer and Emery work together, its clear that the sparks flying between them aren't all from their friendly competition over a job. Will Emery and Archer be able to navigate the ranch, their close quarters, and their individual circumstances to find love this holiday season?

Second Chance Ranch: A Three Rivers Ranch Romance (Book 1): After his deployment, injured and discharged Major Squire Ackerman returns to Three Rivers Ranch, wanting to forgive Kelly for ignoring him a decade ago. He'd like to provide the stable life she needs, but with old wounds opening and a ranch on the brink of financial collapse, it will take patience and faith to make their second chance possible.

Third Time's the Charm: A Three Rivers Ranch Romance (Book 2): First Lieutenant Peter Marshall has a truckload of debt and no way to provide for a family, but Chelsea helps him see past all the obstacles, all the scars. With so many unknowns, can Pete and Chelsea develop the love, acceptance, and faith needed to find their happily ever after?

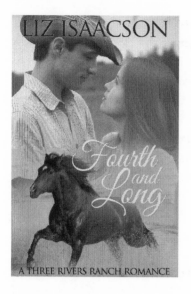

Fourth and Long: A Three Rivers Ranch Romance (Book 3): Commander Brett Murphy goes to Three Rivers Ranch to find some rest and relaxation with his Army buddies. Having his ex-wife show up with a seven-year-old she claims is his son is anything but the R&R he craves. Kate needs to make amends, and Brett needs to find forgiveness, but are they too late to find their happily ever after?

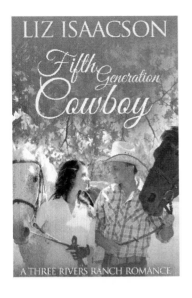

Fifth Generation Cowboy: A Three Rivers Ranch Romance (Book 4): Tom Lovell has watched his friends find their true happiness on Three Rivers Ranch, but everywhere he looks, he only sees friends. Rose Reyes has been bringing her daughter out to the ranch for equine therapy for months, but it doesn't seem to be working. Her challenges with Mari are just as frustrating as ever. Could Tom be exactly what Rose needs? Can he remove his friendship blinders and find love with someone who's been right in front of him all this time?

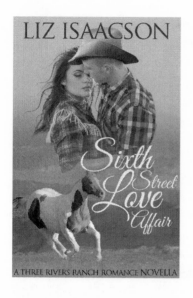

Sixth Street Love Affair: A Three Rivers Ranch Romance (Book 5): After losing his wife a few years back, Garth Ahlstrom thinks he's ready for a second chance at love. But Juliette Thompson has a secret that could destroy their budding relationship. Can they find the strength, patience, and faith to make things work?

The Seventh Sergeant: A Three Rivers Ranch Romance (Book 6): Life has finally started to settle down for Sergeant Reese Sanders after his devastating injury overseas. Discharged from the Army and now with a good job at Courage Reins, he's finally found happiness—until a horrific fall puts him right back where he was years ago: Injured and depressed. Carly Watters, Reese's new veteran care coordinator, dislikes small towns almost as much as she loathes cowboys. But she finds herself faced with both when she gets assigned to Reese's case. Do they have the humility and faith to make their relationship more than professional?

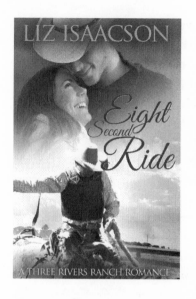

Eight Second Ride: A Three Rivers Ranch Romance (Book 7): Ethan Greene loves his work at Three Rivers Ranch, but he can't seem to find the right woman to settle down with. When sassy yet vulnerable Brynn Bowman shows up at the ranch to recruit him back to the rodeo circuit, he takes a different approach with the barrel racing champion. His patience and newfound faith pay off when a friendship--and more--starts with Brynn. But she wants out of the rodeo circuit right when Ethan wants to rejoin. Can they find the path God wants them to take and still stay together?

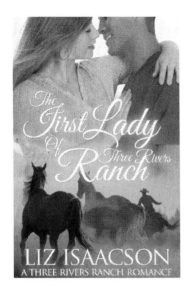

The First Lady of Three Rivers Ranch: A Three Rivers Ranch Romance (Book 8): Heidi Duffin has been dreaming about opening her own bakery since she was thirteen years old. She scrimped and saved for years to afford baking and pastry school in San Francisco. And now she only has one year left before she's a certified pastry chef. Frank Ackerman's father has recently retired, and he's taken over the largest cattle ranch in the Texas Panhandle. A horseman through and through, he's also nearing thirty-one and looking for someone to bring love and joy to a homestead that's been dominated by men for a decade. But when he convinces Heidi to come clean the cowboy cabins, she changes all that. But the siren's call of a bakery is still loud in Heidi's ears, even if she's also seeing a future with Frank. Can she rely on her faith in ways she's never had to before or will their relationship end when summer does?

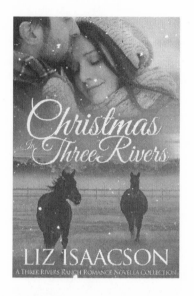

Christmas in Three Rivers: A Three Rivers Ranch Romance (Book 9): Isn't Christmas the best time to fall in love? The cowboys of Three Rivers Ranch think so. Join four of them as they journey toward their path to happily ever after in four, all-new novellas in the Amazon #1 Bestselling Three Rivers Ranch Romance series.

THE NINTH INNING: The Christmas season has never felt like such a burden to boutique owner Andrea Larsen. But with Mama gone and the holidays upon her, Andy finds herself wishing she hadn't been so quick to judge her former boyfriend, cowboy Lawrence Collins. Well, Lawrence hasn't forgotten about Andy either, and he devises a plan to get her out to the ranch so they can reconnect. Do they have the faith and humility to patch things up and start a new relationship?

TEN DAYS IN TOWN: Sandy Keller is tired of the dating scene in Three Rivers. Though she owns the pancake house, she's looking for a fresh start, which means an escape from the town where she grew up. When her older brother's best friend, Tad Jorgensen, comes to town for the holidays, it is a balm to his weary soul. A helicopter tour guide who experienced a near-death experience, he's looking to start over too--but in Three Rivers. Can Sandy and Tad navigate their troubles to find the path God wants them to take--and discover true love--in only ten days?

ELEVEN YEAR REUNION: Pastry chef extraordinaire, Grace

Lewis has moved to Three Rivers to help Heidi Ackerman open a bakery in Three Rivers. Grace relishes the idea of starting over in a town where no one knows about her failed cupcakery. She doesn't expect to run into her old high school boyfriend, Jonathan Carver. A carpenter working at Three Rivers Ranch, Jon's in town against his will. But with Grace now on the scene, Jon's thinking life in Three Rivers is suddenly looking up. But with her focus on baking and his disdain for small towns, can they make their eleven year reunion stick?

THE TWELFTH TOWN: Newscaster Taryn Tucker has had enough of life on-screen. She's bounced from town to town before arriving in Three Rivers, completely alone and completely anonymous--just the way she now likes it. She takes a job cleaning at Three Rivers Ranch, hoping for a chance to figure out who she is and where God wants her. When she meets happy-go-lucky cowhand Kenny Stockton, she doesn't expect sparks to fly. Kenny's always been "the best friend" for his female friends, but the pull between him and Taryn can't be denied. Will they have the courage and faith necessary to make their opposite worlds mesh?

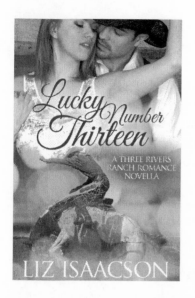

Lucky Number Thirteen: A Three Rivers Ranch Romance (Book 10): Tanner Wolf, a rodeo champion ten times over, is excited to be riding in Three Rivers for the first time since he left his philandering ways and found religion. Seeing his old friends Ethan and Brynn is therapuetic--until a terrible accident lands him in the hospital. With his rodeo career over, Tanner thinks maybe he'll stay in town--and it's not just because his nurse, Summer Hamblin, is the prettiest woman he's ever met. But Summer's the queen of first dates, and as she looks for a way to make a relationship with the transient rodeo star work Summer's not sure she has the fortitude to go on a second date. Can they find love among the tragedy?

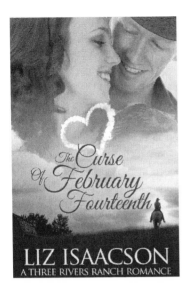

The Curse of February Fourteenth: A Three Rivers Ranch Romance (Book 11): Cal Hodgkins, cowboy veterinarian at Bowman's Breeds, isn't planning to meet anyone at the masked dance in small-town Three Rivers. He just wants to get his bachelor friends off his back and sit on the sidelines to drink his punch. But when he sees a woman dressed in gorgeous butterfly wings and cowgirl boots with blue stitching, he's smitten. Too bad she runs away from the dance before he can get her name, leaving only her boot behind...

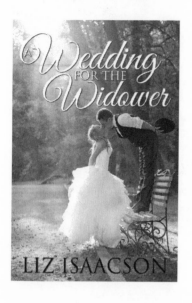

A Companion for the Cowboy: Brush Creek Brides Romance (Book 2): Cowboy and professional roper Justin Jackman has found solitude at Brush Creek Horse Ranch, preferring his time with the animals he trains over dating. With two failed engagements in his past, he's not really interested in getting his heart stomped on again. But when flirty and fun Renee Martin picks him up at a church ice cream bar--on a bet, no less--he finds himself more than just a little interested. His Gen-X attitudes are attractive to her; her Millennial behaviors drive him nuts. Can Justin look past their differences and take a chance on another engagement?

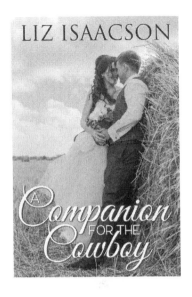

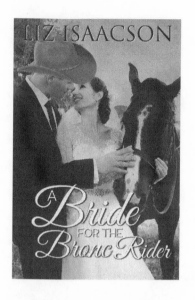

A Bride for the Bronc Rider: Brush Creek Brides Romance (Book 3): Ted Caldwell has been a retired bronc rider for years, and he thought he was perfectly happy training horses to buck at Brush Creek Ranch. He was wrong. When he meets April Nox, who comes to the ranch to hide her pregnancy from all her friends back in Jackson Hole, Ted realizes he has a huge family-shaped hole in his life. April is embarrassed, heartbroken, and trying to find her extinguished faith. She's never ridden a horse and wants nothing to do with a cowboy ever again. Can Ted and April create a family of happiness and love from a tragedy?

A Family for the Farmer: Brush Creek Brides Romance (Book 4): Blake Gibbons oversees all the agriculture at Brush Creek Horse Ranch, sometimes moonlighting as a general contractor. When he meets Erin Shields, new in town, at her aunt's bakery, he's instantly smitten. Erin moved to Brush Creek after a divorce that left her penniless, homeless, and a single mother of three children under age eight. She's nowhere near ready to start dating again, 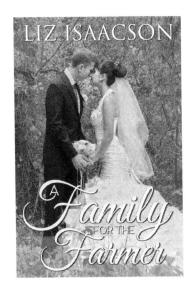 but the longer Blake hangs around the bakery, the more she starts to like him. Can Blake and Erin find a way to blend their lifestyles and become a family?

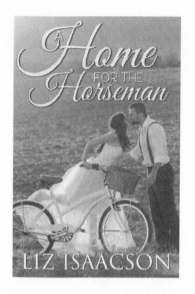

A Home for the Horseman: Brush Creek Brides Romance (Book 5): Emmett Graves has always had a positive outlook on life. He adores training horses to become barrel racing champions during the day and cuddling with his cat at night. Fresh off her professional rodeo retirement, Molly Brady comes to Brush Creek Horse Ranch as Emmett's protege. He's not thrilled, and she's allergic to cats. Oh, and she'd like to stay cowboy-free, thank you very much. But Emmett's about as cowboy as they come.... Can Emmett and Molly work together without falling in love?

A Refuge for the Rancher: Brush Creek Brides Romance (Book 6): Grant Ford spends his days training cattle—when he's not camped out at the elementary school hoping to catch a glimpse of his ex-girlfriend. When principal Shannon Sharpe confronts him and asks him to stay away from the school, the spark between them is instant and hot. Shannon's expecting a transfer very soon, but she also needs a summer outdoor coordinator— 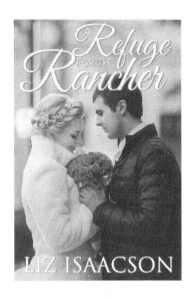 and Grant fits the bill. Just because he's handsome and everything Shannon's ever wanted in a cowboy husband means nothing. Will Grant and Shannon be able to survive the summer or will the Utah heat be too much for them to handle?

ABOUT LIZ

Liz Isaacson writes inspirational romance, usually set in Texas, or Montana, or anywhere else horses and cowboys exist. She lives in Utah, where she teaches elementary school, taxis her daughter to dance several times a week, and eats a lot of Ferrero Rocher while writing. Find her on her website at lizisaacson.com.

Made in the USA
Monee, IL
10 July 2022

99429421R00134